Striptease

GEORGES SIMENON

Striptease

Translated by Robert Brain

A Helen and Kurt Wolff Book
Harcourt Brace Jovanovich, Publishers
San Diego   New York   London

Striptease was first published (under the same title)
in France in 1958.

Library of Congress Cataloging-in-Publication Data
Simenon, Georges, 1903–
[Striptease. English]
Striptease / Georges Simenon ; translated by Robert Brain.—1st ed.
p. cm.
Translation of: Striptease.
"A Helen and Kurt Wolff book."
ISBN 0-15-185910-8
I. Title.
PQ2637.I53S7713   1989
843'.912—dc19   89-30844

Design by Kaelin Chappell
Printed in the United States of America

First United States edition

A B C D E

Part One

Part One

Chapter One

Célita was the first to see the new girl.

As usual at three o'clock in the afternoon, she had heard the alarm clock go off on the little table between the two beds and, curling up in the sheets, had left Marie-Lou to stop the ringing and, next, to get up and open the shutters, bring in the nylons and brassieres that were drying on the window ledge, and light the small kitchen gas stove to make coffee.

Marie-Lou liked to sleep naked and always spent a long time wandering around the three small rooms of the flat, even when the windows were open, without dreaming of putting on any clothes. There was no sun today: the sky was overcast, the light bluish green, which meant it would rain.

"Aren't you ever going to get up?"

When, for reasons of economy, they had first decided to share the flat, they planned to take turns getting breakfast, but, confronted with Célita's complete inertia, Marie-Lou had resigned herself to doing it almost every day.

In the mornings her skin had an oily look, and it was perhaps because of that that she looked somehow fatter, grosser, particularly when the light exaggerated her skin's irregularities, the bluish patch under her arms where she shaved, and a brown wart just below her left breast. Like many fat people, she felt no embarrassment as she traipsed from the bedroom to the living room and the narrow kitchen, indifferent to the fact that her heavy nakedness could be seen from the windows opposite.

That day Célita could only be bothered to have a quick shower, and, with her hair tied in a ponytail, she hurriedly pulled on her clothes, which had been scattered on chairs and over the floor.

"Going out?"

"I've got to sew up my red dress. Some lout ripped it again last night, trying to grab hold of me as I went past him."

This meant that Marie-Lou would be left to do all the housework again, just as she had been left to get the breakfast. All Célita did was bring in the milk and bread from outside the door.

The fat girl hardly ever complained, and Célita, instead of showing any gratitude, rather despised her for it; once she said to Natasha:

"She's still nothing but a maid at heart!"

Marie-Lou had indeed been a housemaid for more than three years.

Célita walked briskly through the streets of Cannes, where people had already begun the second half of their day. She wore a thin pair of ballerina shoes and had a green coat thrown across her shoulders.

She made a detour to buy a piece of red silk, and in the small triangular square in front of the church of Notre-Dame she was held up by a crowd of curious onlookers, drawn up in two ranks for a wedding group to pass between. She watched with the rest, even stood on tiptoe to do so.

The bride was wearing a white dress with a train and a veil, and the groom, in a morning suit, held a top hat in his hand, just as in the photographs in magazines.

From the semidarkness of the church, the rumbling of an organ could be heard, and suddenly some girls ran forward to fling handfuls of rice at the couple, who were being kept on the steps by the photographers. And all the while, the women outside were dabbing at their eyes with handkerchiefs.

Did she suddenly feel left out of all this, or was it only a moment of depression that hit her? Her eyelids felt hot and began to smart, and just when everything and everyone about her was becoming blurred, she recognized, in the row of faces opposite her, a man with gray hair she had noticed two or three times at the Monico, although he had never spoken to her. She didn't know whether he lived in town or was a tourist. All he had done was sit on a barstool and stare at her.

Nevertheless, she was sure he had just recognized her, even with her hair untidy and with no makeup on, and, furthermore, that he had seen the signs of emotion, of which she now felt ashamed.

She hated his looking at her like that, so kindly, almost pitying her, and she felt like sticking her tongue out at him. She walked away from the line of people, crossly, shoving aside those in her way, who then followed her with their eyes.

The Monico was only a couple of hundred yards away, not far from the harbor, in a narrow street crowded with cars, which were parked there all day. The door was open, and when Célita pulled the door curtain aside, she found the two charwomen, Madame Blanc and old Madame Touzelli, sweeping up the paper streamers and little colored balls. The atmosphere was still saturated with the smell of champagne and whisky.

Above the garnet-red benches, the window, which was always hidden in the evening by heavy curtains, was now wide open, and the cabaret stage in daylight looked as incongruous as Marie-Lou's nakedness when she made the coffee in their flat.

Célita was surprised that the proprietor, Monsieur Léon, wasn't there when she came in, since most of his afternoons were spent at the Monico. When she pushed open the door leading to the cloakroom at the end of the bar, she saw the trapdoor open and realized he was busy in the cellar.

She climbed the spiral staircase, which she had climbed up and down countless times in the last few months, and reached the empty, low-ceilinged room the girls used as their dressing room.

She rarely went there during the day, and it was strange to see the yard below, where a man from the brewery was stacking barrels. Dresses in different colors and different styles hung from a rod. She unhooked hers, a red Spanish dancer's and, throwing her coat off her shoulders, sat down on a stool and started sewing.

After a while, she thought of Natasha and of the box of American face powder a Navy officer had brought her. The expensive-looking box stood on the long dressing table, where all the girls kept their personal things, and Célita opened the window, emptied her compact into the yard, then filled it to the brim with Natasha's powder.

She didn't stop to ask herself if it was unhappiness or sheer bad temper, yet her face, now that she was sewing again, was as clouded as the sky. She knew that it made her features even more pointed, her eyes more cunning, that she looked like an animal, frightened by a storm, ready to scratch. She hated sewing, just as she hated housework. In fact, there were quite a number of things she hated doing! . . .

She heard a noise downstairs, and through an odd kind of fanlight that had been fitted flush with the floor she saw the proprietor and Emile climbing up from the cellar, each of them carrying bottles of whisky.

"Stack them in the cupboard," Monsieur Léon said.

He put his down on the table and pushed open the bar door, while Emile, noticing Célita looking through the pane of glass, gave a smile of happy surprise and winked at her.

Célita was aware of what went on in the basement: they had been filling empty whisky bottles with contraband whisky. It was none of her business, but she would not be very upset if the proprietor were caught, for she loathed cheats. If she cheated a little herself, it was because she had to, and she loathed herself for it.

There was no point in thinking about it. She finished her work and bit off the thread. The skirt, which she had worn every evening for the past three years, was becoming threadbare and would not last much longer. Its red color looked faded in the daylight. Emile was signaling to her from below, but she couldn't make out what he wanted and half-opened the door to ask:

"What is it?"

He put his finger to his lips and beckoned her to come down quietly.

He was seventeen, but short and puny, so that he looked fifteen, and everybody treated him like a little boy. It was he who helped Monsieur Léon in the afternoons, ran errands and then darted from car to car, putting fliers under the windshield wipers extolling the Monico's floor show.

In the evenings, and up till four o'clock in the morning, he would stand on the sidewalk outside the nightclub, opening car doors, ushering in customers, seeming to float in a uniform much too big for him.

At present he was standing in front of a small window set into the door like a peephole, through which one could see what was going on in the main room.

Célita had missed the beginning, but not much of it, to judge from the conversation she overheard. The two char-women were still cleaning. In the center of the stage, bright with daylight, stood a young girl, looking frightened, not the sort of girl one would expect to find here. She would have been more at home among the people who had been watching the wedding a while ago.

Monsieur Léon was leaning on the bar, his jacket off and his shirtsleeves rolled up above his hairy wrists. He was ap-praising the girl with a slow, heavy look.

"Who sent you here?"

"Nobody did, sir. I just came on my own."

Emile gave Célita a nudge with his elbow; he had moved aside to make room for her at the peephole and was obviously pleased to feel her so close to him.

"You come from Bergerac, you say?"

"Yes, monsieur."

"And you heard about the Monico in Bergerac?"

"No. I haven't come straight from there."

She wore a very simple black dress, a red hat, and she had put on a pair of white string gloves, as if she were going to Mass.

"Tell me."

"Tell you what?"

"Where you've been before you came here."

"I went to Toulouse first. There's a cabaret there called the Moulin Bleu."

"I know the one. Did you work there?"

"No."

"Why not?"

She hesitated, blushed, fiddled nervously with her black patent-leather handbag, which looked new and strangely incongruous compared with her other things.

"They didn't want me."

"You really are nineteen?"

"I can show you my identity card."

Her fingers fumbling from nervousness, she opened her bag as if she was not yet used to it, and held her identity card out to the proprietor, who read, half-aloud:

"Maud Leroy, born May 13 . . ."

"You see!"

"I see. And after Toulouse?"

"I went to Marseille by train and worked as a waitress in a bar for a week."

"Which one?"

"Freddy's Bar."

"Have you been to bed with Freddy?"

Emile gave another nudge with his elbow; Monsieur Léon seemed more than ever like an enormous cat playing with a mouse.

"Who told you that?"

"Freddy's a friend of mine. And before that?"

"What do you mean?"

"How many men have you slept with?"

She was obviously telling the truth when she answered:

"Two."

Célita realized that her breast was pushing into Emile's shoulder, but she didn't move.

"Did Freddy tell you about me?"

"No. It was a customer. I left Bergerac because I wanted to become a striptease dancer, so . . ."

"Why?"

Disconcerted by the question, she could not think of an answer.

"Do you think it's an easy thing to do?"

"I think I could do it."

"When did you arrive in Cannes?"

"I came this morning, on the night train. I called here once before, at eleven, but the door was locked. I've taken a room at the Hôtel de la Poste."

"Take your dress off."

"Now?"

He answered with a shrug of his shoulders, and the girl looked anxiously at the two charwomen, who were apparently taking no notice of her.

"What are you waiting for?"

"Nothing . . ."

At last she made up her mind. First she put her handbag down on the table. She managed to force a smile to her lips, and slowly, keeping her eyes glued to Monsieur Léon, began to take off her black dress, over her head, just as she would have in her bedroom.

"Never over your head! The other way. A woman with her arms in the air and her head inside a dress looks plain awkward."

"I didn't know."

"You'll learn."

"Do I have to take my slip off too?"

Emile took advantage of this to press even harder against Célita, as if he wanted to see better, and she pretended not to notice.

The young girl's slip had fallen around her feet, and now she wore only a bra and panties; her bare skin was an almost chalky white against the nightclub's somber red walls. Célita began to resent the nature of this undressing in broad daylight, with the street noises coming in through the window.

"You don't shave your armpits?"

"Do I have to?"

"Of course you have to! Let's have a look at your breasts."

Her nipples were still smooth and bright pink. Leaning heavily on the bar, Monsieur Léon looked more like a horse dealer than a voyeur, yet Célita couldn't help muttering:

"Filthy bastard!"

At the same moment she shifted a little away from Emile, who, embarrassed, stopped looking through the peephole with quite the same concentration.

"You can put your clothes on now."

"Aren't I any good?"

"I told you to put your clothes on. Have you read the notice by the door?"

As she adjusted the straps of her slip, she nodded her head.

"Every Friday, in addition to our usual show, we have a striptease competition for amateurs. Come here a little before ten o'clock, and sit down at this table. . . ."

He pointed to a table at the front, near the band.

"Behave as if you are a customer, and when the master of ceremonies invites you, stand up as if you are hesitating. Do you understand?"

"And afterward?"

"Don't worry about that. That's up to me. If it comes off, you're hired."

When she had her clothes on again, she looked more than ever like an innocent young girl, and it was hard to believe that she had just stripped without a murmur.

"Thank you."

"All right. Ten o'clock, no later."

"Yes."

"Without fail."

"Without fail."

Just as she pulled the velvet curtain aside to go out, he called her back roughly.

"Have you got any money for supper?"

She turned around, blushed again.

"I don't need anything."

"How much money do you have left?"

"Two hundred francs."

"You'd better take this on account."

He held out a five-hundred-franc note, which she slipped into her handbag.

Emile had already moved away on tiptoe. Célita went back up the iron staircase to fetch her handbag, and when she passed through the main room, the proprietor was listening to the race results on a small radio that was hidden behind the counter.

"Where have you been?"

"Upstairs. I came in to sew up my Spanish skirt."

He studied her suspiciously; they knew each other well, and he was used to her lying.

"There'll be a new girl in tonight," he announced, as if to test her.

"So much the better; it was getting a little dull. Dancer?"

"Striptease."

"Has Madame Florence engaged her?"

It was a low trick, reminding him that it was his wife, whom everybody called "Madame Florence," who was the real boss.

He didn't answer, but if the bar had not been between them, he might easily have slapped her. It had happened before, and yet he was incapable of doing without her. And would Célita, for her part, have been glad to do without him?

At that moment she despised and hated him, because she was scared, as she was each time a new girl appeared, as scared as Madame Florence was.

She went out without saying good-bye and retraced her steps to Place du Commandant-Maria, where she lived with Marie-Lou. Marie-Lou had finished tidying up the flat and was now stretched out on the sofa, filing her nails.

"There's going to be a new girl tonight."

"Who?"

"Nobody. Just a kid who turned up here on the train this morning."

"She'll be like the rest of them."

She wasn't the first, and no doubt she wouldn't be the last, to be tried out this way. Some of them stayed for a single evening only, and there had even been one who had panicked at the last moment, before walking onto the floor, and had run and locked herself in the lavatory.

Most of them wanted to go further than the professionals, but were so clumsy and crude about it that it became obscene and made the customers feel uneasy. Two of three had lasted for a few days. One, a little Italian girl, had got herself installed in a suite at the Carlton by the end of a week.

"Did you see her?"

"Yes."

After a silence, during which Marie-Lou went on filing her nails, the fat girl murmured:

"Is that all?"

"What do you mean?"

"I'm just surprised you've got nothing nasty to say about her."

"Thanks."

"It's a pleasure."

These two understood each other.

At half past eight, wearing the dresses they always wore for dancing with customers of the club between numbers, they were mingling with the crowds in front of brightly lit shop windows, walking precariously on their high heels. For most of the passersby the day was over. A few couples, one or two families, were going into the movie houses.

They found Natasha and Ketty already eating supper at Justin's bar-restaurant on Place du Marché; they also shared a flat, for the same reason: economy.

"Spaghetti, Justin!" Célita called out as she walked past the counter.

They ate here almost every evening and were well known to the other customers, mostly shopkeepers from the neighborhood and, during the night, truck drivers, butchers, farmers who brought their vegetables to market in small trucks.

It was Marie-Lou's turn to announce the news this time.

"It seems there's a new girl."

Oddly enough, they looked at Célita, as if she inevitably knew all about it.

"What's she like?" asked Natasha.

And Célita, pursing her lips, said:

"Just the sort to send one of us packing. We'll soon see who."

It was drizzling now, and because the sidewalk was not very wide, they walked two by two, like schoolgirls, their heads lowered, not talking. When they turned the street corner, it was half past nine. The Monico's sign was not yet lighted. Nevertheless, there was a middle-aged man standing there with his face pressed up against the glass of the display box, staring at the photographs in the gleam of the streetlight.

The four women were about thirty yards from him when the sign and the box containing the pictures were suddenly illuminated. The man, revealed by the light, jumped back, surprised, ashamed, and strode hurriedly away.

"Did you see that?" Marie-Lou inquired.

"What of it?"

"Nothing."

Emile burst out the door, wearing his uniform with epaulettes and braid on it, and stationed himself by the curb. Inside, Madame Florence was already at the cash register, while Ludo, the bartender, was arranging his bottles on the shelves.

"Good evening, Madame Florence."

"Good evening."

"Good evening, Madame Florence."

"Good evening."

They filed past her, as if past the mother superior at a convent, and they felt the same schoolgirl fears. The musicians were tuning their instruments.

"Marie-Lou!"

"Yes, madame."

"Your nails?"

Triumphantly, Marie-Lou held out her newly manicured hands; the day before, Madame Florence had remarked on her dirty nails.

"And your hair?"

It was visibly greasy and, up closer, little white specks of dandruff could be seen.

"I couldn't get an appointment at the hairdresser's today. I'll go tomorrow."

"Without fail, then."

Natasha and Ketty were going through the cloakroom, and Célita was about to follow them when she was also called back.

"Célita!"

"Yes, Madame Florence."

"It seems you were here this afternoon?"

Emile would never have told her; Emile worshiped Célita with a schoolboy's ardor. When he had called her down to look through the peephole with him that afternoon, it was more to feel her close to him than to let her share in the fun.

And it would not have been in Léon's interest, considering their relationship, to say anything.

Had Madame Florence stopped in the Monico before the

two charwomen had gone home? She often did, and somehow or other nothing escaped her.

"I forgot to take my skirt home with me yesterday. A customer grabbed it and tore it. I came in to sew it up again."

Unlike Marie-Lou, Célita did not look down at the floor, but straight at Madame Florence with a slightly mocking twist at the corners of her lips.

"See that it doesn't happen again."

"Very well, Madame Florence."

The irony was obvious. It was a kind of game they had been playing for months. But it was still difficult to pick the eventual winner. The only certain thing at present was that one of them was the proprietress, Monsieur Léon's legal wife, and the other was not.

"Well, why are you standing there?"

"I didn't know you had finished."

Madame Florence could not fail to know about her husband's visits to Place du Commandant-Maria, on the afternoons when Marie-Lou was out shopping. Léon certainly had done the same with others, with nearly all of them, in fact, but this time it had lasted longer, it was somehow different.

He took no notice of Célita at the Monico, or if he did, it was almost always to nag her. Yet he didn't do so to fool Madame Florence, but probably because he often found himself hating the dancer.

Outside in the street, Emile, a red umbrella in his hand, rushed toward a car that had stopped. He was on the point of opening the door when the driver, who was only lighting a cigarette, drove off again. Disappointed, he went back to his post by the entrance, where he could hear the band. It was rather like fishing. Some days were good, some bad. And every time a car came around the corner, Emile felt the same little tug at his heart as a fisherman feels when his float sinks.

"The show will be starting right away, ladies and gentlemen. . . ."

"When does that mean?"

He never dared lie too openly. The show rarely started before midnight; sometimes later, if there were not enough people.

Some of them pulled aside the red curtain, and when they saw the empty room, turned away, in spite of the fact that the band would strike up, as if at a signal.

"We'll come back later. . . ."

"You'd better reserve a table. . . ."

On the other hand, a miracle sometimes happened: in the space of a few minutes, the place would be so full that clients were jammed around the bar.

In their dressing room upstairs, the four women were putting on their makeup; Natasha, almost at once, turned to Célita and asked:

"Did you pinch my powder?"

Célita didn't answer. The others paid hardly any attention to them.

"If you'd only asked me, I'd have given you some. But . . ."

She grabbed hold of Célita's handbag, took out her compact, and threw the contents in the wastepaper basket, on top of a pile of soiled cotton balls.

Her action provoked no protest from Célita, who simply gave her a hard, penetrating look as she went on brushing her hair.

Somebody was hurrying by outside, along the dark street,

the rhythmic sound of her high heels disturbing the silence of the night. Emile looked at his watch, and when the woman passed him, he murmured, with a touch of anxiety in his voice:

"Hurry up, Mademoiselle Francine!"

She was a pretty girl, plump and fresh, with curly hair. She went no farther than the bar, and was aware that everybody was staring at her: Ludo, the musicians, Jules, who was placing champagne buckets on the tables.

"I'm terribly sorry, Madame Florence. I'm a little late. . . ."

"Eleven minutes."

Without waiting, the proprietress had taken a notebook from the drawer, with a list of the employees' names, some of them with check marks after them.

"It's because the woman next door, the one who keeps an eye on my little boy in the evenings, hadn't come home and I couldn't leave Pierrot. . . ."

"I'm sorry, Francine."

A mark was added to three others already there, each of which meant five hundred francs off Francine's wages.

"I ran as quickly as I could. . . ."

It was true. She was still panting.

"Go and take your coat off."

Francine was not a singer or a dancer, performed no part in the show. She was a dance hostess and, on top of that, was in charge of the cloakroom, hanging up customers' coats and hats in the recess.

Monsieur Léon arrived at five minutes to ten and sat on a stool at the bar, looking around to make sure that everything was in order.

"Are the hats ready?" he asked Jules, the waiter.

Every evening they handed out party hats made of paper

and cardboard, sometimes cowboy hats, sometimes sailors' berets or top hats, in all colors.

"Do you think she'll come?" his wife asked; he had told her about the new girl.

"I'm certain she will."

Eventually Emile led in two customers, who were about to sit at the bar when Francine rushed up to show them to a table. Once there, they were caught.

Almost immediately afterward, Maud Leroy, the girl who had come that afternoon, pushed her way through the double thickness of red velvet and stood there a moment, confused, having some difficulty recognizing the room.

Madame Florence was also a little taken aback, because the new girl was not the kind they were used to at the Monico. With a frown, she glanced at her husband out of the corner of her eye, as if she were trying to figure something out.

It was Ludo, the bartender, who called out:

"There's a good table in the front, mademoiselle."

Another customer appeared, a regular, who sat down on the stool at the end of the bar, his back to the wall.

"Scotch, Ludo."

"Coming up, doctor."

He called almost all of them "doctor," and some were flattered by it.

Madame Florence half-opened the door of the cloakroom, right next to the cash register, and called up the iron staircase:

"Are you ready there?"

Instantly there was a sound of activity. Natasha and Ketty went down first. As she started down the stairs, Marie-Lou asked:

"Did you really pinch her powder?"

Célita looked at her expressionlessly and merely shrugged her shoulders.

Downstairs, the new girl was sitting bolt upright at her table, looking at a glass of yellowish liquid that had automatically been brought for her. Ketty, who was almost as fat as Marie-Lou, though more aggressive, more sensually coarse, walked over to the two men.

"Isn't anybody going to ask me to dance?"

Natasha, standing near the bar, waited to follow her.

Célita and Marie-Lou appeared, and all that remained to be done was to "get in the mood," to create the right atmosphere.

Emile, triumphant, suddenly flung aside the curtain and let in, not one couple, but three couples at once, a party of Dutch people, terribly sunburned in spite of the dull weather of the last few days.

Five minutes later, Gianini, the bandleader, was barking out the words of the tunes' refrains through his megaphone, and everybody was dancing on the tiny floor, colliding with each other.

At half past eleven, three-quarters of the tables were occupied, and Madame Florence called out in a low voice, giving the signal:

"Ketty! Marie-Lou!"

It was time for them to go and dress for their numbers. The other two, plus Francine, continued as dancing partners until they were ready.

Only the new girl had not danced, and none of the customers had yet dared address a word to her.

The girls had been able to examine her at their leisure as they danced or drank at the bar; so had the musicians and Ludo, who had sent a drink across to her three times. She had drunk mechanically, for the sake of appearances, and although she still sat as stiffly on her chair as during a sermon in church, her face was not quite so pale.

Madame Florence, without missing a thing that happened in the room, had looked across at Léon more often than usual.

She would soon be forty, and the struggle was becoming too much for her.

Chapter Two

She was curled up in bed like a dog, the sheet twisted around her body to such an extent that all that could be seen of her was a mass of tawny hair, one temple, one eye staring at the strips of light through the shutters. Occasionally her glance, turning without a sound or a move on her part, shifted to the next bed, or to the alarm clock, although its dial faced the other way.

Célita did not know what time it was, but she was sure that the bell would soon start ringing, and when at last it did, and the legs of the alarm clock began to vibrate on the marble-topped table, she shut her eyes at once, and at the same time her face assumed an exaggerated expression of innocent, yet sulky sleep, while Marie-Lou's heavy warm body slowly came to life and her arm reached out in semidarkness.

Without looking, Célita knew her friend was sitting on the edge of her bed, her feet fumbling around on the floor for her slippers, and then, rubbing her breasts and waist, wandering out of the bedroom to the kitchen to light the stove, which made its usual little pop.

When Marie-Lou had opened the windows and the shutters in the living room, sunshine invaded the flat and the noises from Place du Commandant-Maria became more distinct.

Through her barely parted eyelashes, Célita watched the fat girl, who returned to the room after leaning out the window, grabbed a gaudy dressing gown, which she wrapped around her before setting off again, raised her head and called out:

"Is Pierrot better?"

She was speaking to Francine, who lived in the house opposite, on the second floor; her boy had been home from school with a cold.

"What did you say?" Marie-Lou called again, after a silence; the din made by a truck had drowned out the reply.

Francine repeated herself, adding:

"He's at school. I was waiting for you to get up to ask you to do me a favor."

There was a dairy at the corner, and customers there would be noticing, through the bead curtain, these two women who were just getting up at three o'clock in the afternoon.

"What kind of favor?"

"Could you look after him for me between four and six?"

Francine's five-year-old son quite often came and spent the afternoon at Marie-Lou and Célita's flat, or else one of them took him to the beach.

He was big for his age, with red cheeks and blond hair; he would have looked pudding-faced or sleepy but for the sparkle that could be seen through the narrow slits of his eyelids.

"I'm sorry," Marie-Lou answered, "I can't today. I've got an appointment at the hairdresser's."

"What about Célita?" the distant voice asked.

Through the open door between the two rooms, Marie-Lou glanced at the bed and saw the disheveled head on the pillow. She lowered her voice and, with a gesture of her hand which must have meant something, replied:

"Better not . . . You understand? . . ."

Francine must indeed have understood, since she didn't press the matter.

"I've got to go inside now. The water's boiling."

Célita continued to pretend she was sleeping and soon smelled the coffee being made. She heard the door close, the crack of a thin piece of bread being broken, a cup clink against a saucer.

Marie-Lou was taking care not to wake her, and Célita was not going to make the first move; so she remained in bed, quite still.

She had a guilty conscience, but, instead of facing it, she was feeling bitter toward her friend for what she considered a betrayal. The night before, or, rather, that morning, as they came home from the Monico together, Marie-Lou hadn't once opened her mouth, and she had undressed right away and gone to bed without saying good night.

It was going to be worse with the others; Célita was expecting it. Anyway, they hated her already. A little more or less, what did it matter?

And was the celebrated Maud, the new girl, also waking up at this moment, in her bedroom at the Hôtel de la Poste? Had Monsieur Léon already been knocking at her door?

Madame Florence was the only one who had not reacted like the rest, and for a brief moment, as Célita's eyes had chanced to meet hers, a look of understanding, tinged with complicity, had passed between them.

Although their positions were dissimilar, they would both defend themselves, and in each case the same man was involved.

Nothing had been premeditated. Célita had only done it on the spur of the moment, although she was aware that she was playing a dirty trick. She was not drunk. She had had three or four glasses of whisky at the most, and, God knows, the ones Ludo poured were short measure, particularly when he served the hostesses.

A few minutes before midnight, having peered through the peephole to make sure Ketty was ready in the cloakroom, Madame Florence had given Gianini the signal. When the dance ended, there was a drumroll followed by a crash of cymbals, and then he had made his usual speech:

"Ladies and gentlemen, the management of the Monico has the greatest pleasure in presenting to you their striptease review, the most daring, the most artistic show on all the Riviera. To begin with, here is Mademoiselle Ketty, the incomparable cover girl, in her original number. . . ."

At that moment Célita was sitting at the bar with a young Englishman, who had bought her a drink but would not dance.

As usual, the place was plunged into absolute darkness for Ketty's number. The first flash of a photographer's flare revealed her swathed in black silk, like a girl posing for a magazine cover, a long cigarette holder in her hand.

Darkness. Flash. Darkness . . . Each time, Ketty was sitting in the same place, slightly more undressed, until she finally appeared completely naked except for the regulation G-string.

The Englishman only bothered to give her a quick look and went on talking in labored French about nightclubs in London, where you couldn't buy a drink after eleven o'clock in the evening.

"And now, ladies and gentlemen . . ."

Marie-Lou's turn: her number was cruder and more ordinary. She was also dressed in black. Her dress, her corset, her underclothes were all fastened with zippers, which she invited the customers to undo.

"You're next, Célita. . . ."

She excused herself to the Englishman, walked through the small cloakroom, and climbed the iron staircase. Natasha was busily completing the last stages of a flashy getup, in the style of the early 1900s, topped by a hat trimmed with ostrich feathers.

They could hear snatches of music and applause.

Célita went down in her Spanish costume and, as they each did in turn, watched the end of the previous act through the peephole. Marie-Lou was also now naked, wearing only a G-string, like Ketty, except that hers was covered with spangles, and she was walking across the floor for the last time before collecting her clothes and taking her leave.

When she pushed open the door, breathless, her body was hot, shining with sweat.

"Your turn."

"And now, ladies and gentlemen, I have the pleasure . . ."

She had heard the phrases so many times before that she failed to distinguish the individual words; like horses at the circus, she waited for the first bars of music before going onto the floor.

As she danced a flamenco, at the end of which she would lose her bodice and red skirt, Célita noticed that the Englishman had disappeared, then, a little later, that the new girl, in her corner, was staring fixedly into space.

Célita was the only trained dancer; her mother had enrolled her at a dancing school in Paris when she was eight, and she had been a member of several corps de ballet. She was also the only one not to expose her breasts, even though hers were firmer and higher than Marie-Lou's, for example. Nor did she have a G-string clinging to the skin of her abdomen; both for the Spanish dances and for the cancan, she wore linen pants with flounces.

The club was full for a Friday. Already there was a blanket of smoke hovering overhead, and the comic hats had been distributed. During the show, Monsieur Léon was in his usual position near the door, where he encouraged the applause.

Had Célita won her struggle with him? She was beginning to think so; she fervently hoped so.

Their eyes met for an instant, but she couldn't read anything in his look, apart from a certain impatience, and she was convinced it was on account of Maud.

Like Marie-Lou a little earlier, she hurried off toward the cloakroom, brushing past Natasha, who was waiting for her cue, holding a very long-handled mauve parasol.

Marie-Lou was already downstairs, sitting at the table with the two men who had arrived first; they had offered her a drink at last. In the dressing room, Ketty was getting ready to go down and she merely said:

"Quite a crowd!"

If there were enough people left at two o'clock, they would have to put on a second show, and the whole thing would start again, with Gianini making the same announcements, the girls going up and down the iron staircase, getting dressed and undressed all over again, making excuses as they parted from customers who might or might not be there on their return.

She put on her hostess dress, which was getting worn too, went down, watched, from the cloakroom, the end of Natasha's number, the most intricate and sophisticated of them all. Natasha had a beautiful body, but she was so tall that she looked more like a statue in a square than a woman you would take to bed. Célita hadn't thought that one up. It was a remark made by an Italian who came to Cannes once a month to gamble at the Casino and only appeared in the Monico when he had lost money up to a self-imposed limit earlier in the evening.

Another drumroll, a crash of cymbals, followed by an almost solemn silence, during which Célita slipped into the room and remained standing near the cloakroom door.

"This is Friday night, ladies and gentlemen, and every Friday we have our amateur striptease competition. . . . The management of the Monico is convinced that among our charming spectators there are hidden talents, women and young girls who are burning with the desire to start a career of . . ."

Each week the same old words, the same winks, the same pauses, which Gianini had perfected once and for all. The lights were put out and replaced by a spotlight, which searched the room while he poured out his patter. It stopped from time to time at certain tables, emphatically or merely glancingly, revealing now a face, now a bosom, sometimes legs intertwined.

"Let's see which girl or young lady is going to win the bottle of champagne the management has kindly presented. . . . You, madame?"

He knew he would get a good laugh if he chose one of the lobster-faced Dutch women, who giggled like a child, while her husband teased her, pretending to push her forward.

Célita didn't take her eyes off Maud during all this. The girl sat completely still, her lips drained of all color, her nostrils pinched, seeming to have stopped breathing.

Célita was aware that she wasn't the only one watching her in this way; Madame Florence at the cash register and the proprietor at the door were no less attentive, although for different reasons.

Once, the young girl put her hand out to her bag, as if she were going to seize it and rush into the street. Jules, working the spotlight, must have noticed this movement and suspected the danger, because the light was suddenly swung onto her.

Gianini saw that the time had come.

"You, mademoiselle?"

Like a hunted animal, she remained perfectly still.

"Will you tell me your name?"

Her lips moved, but there was not the slightest sound.

"What did you say? . . . Hortense? . . . Ursule? . . . Pélagie? . . ."

This time the people at the next table heard her murmur something, and one of them repeated in a loud voice:

"Maud."

"What a pretty name, Maud! . . . Well now, Mademoiselle Maud . . . You aren't married, I suppose? . . ."

Did she know what was happening to her? She shook her head, mechanically.

"Will you oblige the ladies and gentlemen by standing up? Then we can all see just how nice you are."

She got to her feet, with an abrupt jerk.

"That's fine! Perfect! You see, you're getting used to it already. Don't be scared. The rest will come quite naturally. How old are you, Maud?"

"Nineteen."

"Nineteen! How marvelous! I want all the other nineteen-year-olds in the audience to raise their little fingers! . . . Nobody? . . . What, sir? Ninety? . . . That's not quite the same, you know. . . . You see, Maud, you're already in a class of your own. . . . Are you engaged?"

"No."

"Louder."

"No!"

"Unfortunate for him, but fortunate for the rest of us, eh? Come closer, Maud . . . Don't be nervous . . . You've just been admiring our pretty girls doing their acts, and now you're going to show us that you needn't have done it for years to be good at it. . . ."

In spite of his glibness and his teasing, he was following all the girl's reactions carefully and he sensed in time her mounting panic. He made a sign to the band, and they understood. After a crash from the bass drum, heavy, rhythmic music accompanied him as he went on talking, insistently, like a hypnotist:

"Come just another two steps closer, Maud . . . two steps . . . I said two steps . . . Of course you can! . . . You see? . . . Very good . . . Ladies and gentlemen, Mademoiselle Maud is now going to perform for you her first striptease act. . . ."

He conducted the band with both hands now, and they played with a strong beat, haunting chords, while the spotlight, turning red, enveloped Maud in a suggestive glow.

The newcomer, with her eyes glued to Gianini, lifted her hands to her shoulders to slip off her dress, but her arms fell down again, weakly, standing out white alongside her body.

He smiled at her, urging her on, still beating time with his hands as if he were carving strange shapes in the air.

Suddenly she glanced fearfully across at the door, where, through a fog of smoke, she saw the proprietor's gaze fixed on her.

The whole thing was becoming painful, and somebody at a table opened his mouth to call out "That's enough! . . ."

At that moment Célita was feeling as embarrassed as the rest, waiting for something that just wasn't happening. Weren't they all conscious of taking part in some cruel game?

The girl's hands were rising again, pink and pale; her fingers moved the straps of her black dress so that they revealed, first, the polished nakedness of her round shoulders, then the hollows of her armpits, her still thin arms.

Her body remained motionless, stiff, while the dress slowly slipped down till, having passed her hips, it fell suddenly around her feet.

One person alone started applauding from a corner. Another hissed: "Ssssh!"

Perhaps the music, like a sort of voodoo incantation, was having a soothing effect on the audience's taut nerves, for no one spoke or touched a glass. Everybody's eyes, without exception, converged on that unmoving silhouette in the now purple spotlight.

Slowly the girl bent down and extricated her legs. Then, probably unconsciously, she did something almost inspired. Her hands gradually moved back up her body, caressing lovingly the silk of her stockings. As she pulled at her slip, she revealed her body little by little, a body that somehow looked more intimate than that of any of the girls who had just preceded her.

Even Gianini was holding his breath now, careful not to break the spell she was casting, trying to match the girl's gestures with his music, encouraging, even provoking them.

Célita's pointed teeth bit into her lip. Twice, three times, she thought, she hoped, that Maud would panic at the last minute, that she would suddenly break off, see the faces watching her and run away.

Nothing like that happened. Ignoring Monsieur Léon's instructions, the girl took off her slip over her head. It was like a sudden deliverance: the feeling of her near-nakedness was like a slap in her face, and the blood rushed to her cheeks as she now took her eyes off the bandleader and dared, at last, to search the darkened room.

There were sighs of relief, particularly when she allowed a smile to flit across her face, a smile directed only at herself, at her own secret thoughts.

Gianini grasped the situation and accelerated the beat until the music throbbed savagely, like a jungle tom-tom.

Then she began to dance. Not a trained dance. It was hardly a dance at all, strictly speaking, but the movements, still hesitant, of a being who was slowly coming to life.

Throughout, everybody could feel that the whole thing was suspended on a thread, that the slightest thing—a cough, a laugh, a noise—would be enough to break the spell.

The hardest part remained to be done. Célita knew that better than anybody, she who had never consented to reveal her breasts in public.

A deep, long breath, a frightened, anxious look into the dark space around her, and Maud slipped one hand behind her back to unfasten her brassiere.

At that instant Célita bit her lip so hard that she felt a drop of blood; she realized the new girl had just won a victory, that neither she nor any of the other girls had ever been able to hold an audience in such breathless suspense.

After another crash of cymbals, Gianini, with beads of sweat on his forehead, abruptly changed the beat again; the instruments made the music seem to pant, hesitatingly at first, plaintively, then little by little almost triumphantly.

Was this what the girl from Bergerac had imagined when she left home determined to become a striptease artist? Were those looks, caressing her body, sending her into a kind of trance?

Unlike Marie-Lou, she did not merely mime the stages of lovemaking. She was living them, defying the people who were watching her. They could see the tremors run across her skin, and men and women alike forgot her breasts, her stomach, her buttocks, to stare into the wild light in her eyes.

When she fell to her knees, everybody stood up, a few applauding. They were quickly silenced, for, eyelids half-closed, her body was undergoing a mysterious struggle until, at last, she fell backward, drained of all strength.

Célita had been as fascinated as the rest of them, but it only made her doubly furious, particularly when the oppressive silence was followed by an ovation that made the glasses jump on the tables. The customers clapped their hands, stamped their feet, called out, stood on tiptoe to peer over other people's shoulders at the girl's body, now so still, as if it had been emptied of all substance.

"Ladies and gentlemen . . ."

Gianini's voice was lost in the din. Anxiously, Monsieur Léon was pushing his way through the crowd, no longer able to see anything from the door.

"Well done, my dear!"

He was so overcome that Célita and Madame Florence glanced at each other.

The proprietor was holding out his hand to Maud, helping

her to get up. He picked up her clothes and led her away to the door with the peephole.

They were still applauding, and Gianini struck up a samba, which attracted many couples onto the floor. The lights had been turned on again.

Madame Florence had left the cash register. She must have gone to join her husband and the girl in the hallway. Natasha muttered, as she walked past:

"So you were right after all, darling. . . ."

Célita remembered that she had told them at Justin's a while ago that the new girl might take the place of one of them. She had said it to tease them, not really believing it.

Maud Leroy threatened to take not merely the place of one of them, but Célita's own particular place. Madame Florence had realized this too. It was all very well to hate each other, to fight over the same man, but nonetheless, in a case like this, they might join forces.

After the first show there was always a certain upheaval. Customers would ask for the bill, and Jules wouldn't know which way to turn, while Francine would hurry to and fro, laden with coats and furs.

Nobody was paying any attention to a black patent-leather handbag lying beside an empty glass on the table where Maud had sat. This bag, which was so new, fascinated Célita, who had already noticed that afternoon how it contrasted with the tired-looking clothes the girl wore.

But it was not intuition, only simple curiosity. Nothing prevented her from going and sitting at the next table; it was unoccupied and it was a place where the girls often sat. Marie-Lou was busy with her two customers. Natasha was standing at the bar trying to persuade an American to buy her a drink; he had just come in and must at first have thought everything was over.

"Bring me a Scotch, Jules."

"In a minute, Mademoiselle Célita. When I've given them their change."

She put the bag on her lap, as if it were her own, and began searching inside. She found an enameled-copper compact, a handkerchief, two letters, a tube of aspirin, some cotton balls, and an almost empty pack of cigarettes.

What made her take one of the three cigarettes left and light it? Sheer defiance? To pay back the new girl for the wrong she was unwittingly doing her?

She slid her fingers down into the small pockets sewn on the inside of the bag and drew out a small rectangular card. Printed on it were the words GALERIES NOUVELLES. And below, stamped in violet ink, the sum *4450 francs*.

When Jules approached, the bag was back in its former place on the table, and Célita was no longer there. She was slipping toward the exit. Emile, who was much occupied with departing customers, noticed her, but had no time to say anything.

A narrow street, too narrow for cars, with old houses without a single light still shining on either side, ran off to the right toward Place du Marché, the market.

A few trucks had already arrived and were beginning to be unloaded. Two men in overalls and leather caps were eating sandwiches and drinking coffee at Justin's bar.

She asked him for a token for the telephone.

He noticed that she looked drawn, that her eyes were feverish, but he thought nothing of it as he watched her walk to the booth.

"Hello! . . . Is that the police? . . . A handbag priced at four thousand four hundred and fifty francs was stolen from the Galeries Nouvelles, on Rue Foch, this morning. . . . The thief is now at the Monico, where she's just done a striptease act. . . . Her name is Maud Leroy."

"Who is speaking?" a voice answered, unimpressed.

She hung up and left the booth, forgetting to shut the door.

"I'll pay you later, Justin."

"Have you got a crowd there?"

When she returned to the Monico, things had calmed down again, and Emile, back on sentry duty, opened his mouth to ask her a question. But she slipped between the velvet curtains before he had time to speak.

Florence, back at the cash register, frowned. The gray-haired man she had noticed that afternoon watching the wedding procession was sitting at the bar, and she went straight to work:

"Will you buy me a drink?"

"If you want me to."

She jerked herself up onto the stool next to his.

"Thanks. Scotch, Ludo."

"Cigarette?" her companion offered.

She took one and lit it.

"Been out for some fresh air?"

For a moment she wondered whether he was making fun of her, he was smiling at her so oddly. She had noticed that smile of his the two or three times he had been there before; it was only a sketch of a smile, but it had been enough to keep her from talking to him. He was too pleased with himself; he studied people with a curiosity that seemed too compassionate.

She remembered saying to Marie-Lou:

"That one thinks he's God the Father!"

Marie-Lou had added, banteringly:

"God the Father watching the girls strip!"

He was soberly dressed, in a tweed suit, and suggested a doctor or a lawyer. Perhaps a professor?

Neither Monsieur Léon nor the new girl was in the room. A little later they appeared together, and the proprietor led the girl to her table, where she found her bag. He left her and went to have a word, first with his wife, then with Gianini, who listened to him while quietly playing his accordion.

The amateur's trick could not be repeated at the second show because too many of the customers who had seen it earlier had stayed on.

Since Maud had not left, but had been given something to drink, it meant that she would appear with the others, although she would presumably be announced as the sensational newcomer.

Provided that . . .

Célita turned and looked toward the door, wondering whether the police had taken her telephone call seriously and if they would send someone.

"Had a bad day?" her companion with the gray hair asked her, in a light tone.

"Why do you think that?"

"You were a bundle of nerves this afternoon. You don't much like watching others getting married, is that it?"

She went on drinking, not answering him. At that moment Emile came in, tried to attract the proprietor's attention, but succeeded only when it was too late and Inspector Moselli, who occasionally called to keep an eye on the Monico, was walking up to the cash register.

"No!" Célita spat at the gray-haired man. "Nothing's the matter with me, do you hear! Just what are you trying to insinuate? . . ."

She realized too late that she had behaved unwisely. Everything was happening too rapidly now. At the end of the counter, the inspector was speaking to Madame Florence in a low voice, and her husband had joined them. The policeman had not entered unnoticed and people were looking in his direction, including Marie-Lou, Natasha, and Francine, sitting alone at a table.

After a moment Monsieur Léon went over to Maud, who mechanically picked up her bag and followed the proprietor into the small cloakroom. The inspector went in after them.

Célita expected the glance, or, rather, the series of glances, that Madame Florence duly gave her; the first furtive, hesitant, as if she was not yet sure what was going on. The second revealed a certain surprise, as if she were thinking:

Well, my girl, I never thought you'd be capable of going as far as that!

An admiring glance? A little, perhaps. Are there not times when we admire, despite ourselves, people who have the courage to do harm?

She probably had an inkling that Célita was actually working for both of them. Yet Célita realized, from the resigned look on the woman's face, that her attempt would hang in the balance.

Natasha, always more curious than the others, was making her way to the cloakroom, pretending to be going to the lavatory.

"What's got you so scared?"

She was beginning to hate this insidious voice, the way the

man in the tweed suit looked at her, sarcastically and yet indulgently.

"Not you, anyway!" she answered dryly.

And she got down from her stool to go and sit with Francine.

"Did you see that?" the latter asked.

"See what?"

"The inspector. He's come for the new one. I wonder what they're up to back there."

They were all to find out a little later. The policeman in due course came back into the room with the proprietor, and they had a drink at the bar. Not until the inspector had gone did Maud come and sit down at her former table, holding her bag in her hand, her eyes moist and her cheeks flushed.

Natasha moved eagerly from one to another of the girls, whispering in their ears and indicating Célita with her glance.

Monsieur Léon must have handed over the money for the handbag, thus making sure they would hear no more of the matter. Had the shop even noticed the theft? It was unlikely. The strangest thing of all was that Célita, even at the moment of discovering the price tag, had realized the girl was not wholly guilty. She probably had only an old bag, hardly presentable enough for the day she was going to take such an important step. She had only two hundred francs left. . . . It was worth the chance.

For the rest of the evening, Monsieur Léon looked right through Célita. When she went upstairs to change for the second show, Natasha ignored her, and later, outside in the street, Marie-Lou was equally disdainful and silent.

She knew what it meant; she was being sent to Coventry, just as she had been at school.

Now Marie-Lou had finished her bath. She came into the bedroom, her body dripping, and without bothering to find out if Célita was awake or not, gathered up her underwear and clothes.

Célita preferred to keep still, her eyes shut, hoping that her friend would not notice the two tears squeezing between her eyelids.

She wasn't even to be allowed to mind Pierrot!

She would be by herself until evening, because Marie-Lou had put on the blue frock she wore to go to the Monico and was obviously planning not to come home first.

The door opened and shut, footsteps faded away along the sidewalk. Célita jumped out of bed, tempted to run and call her friend back.

She had never felt quite so lonely in the three-room flat, where flies were now buzzing in the sunshine and all the noises from outside seemed hostile.

She almost felt she had been caught in a trap.

She lifted the telephone receiver, dialed a number, heard it ringing at the other end of the line, then finally a hesitant voice, the voice of somebody who wasn't used to speaking on the telephone.

"Yes?"

"Is this the Monico?"

"This is the Monico, yes."

She thought she recognized Madame Touzelli's mumbling voice.

"Has Monsieur Léon arrived?"

"No, madame."

"Madame Florence is not there either?"

"There's nobody here."

Angrily she hung up, poured herself a cup of cold coffee, ate nothing, and ran herself a bath. She must get some clothes on as quickly as possible and go out somewhere, along Rue d'Antibes or the Croisette, anywhere, so long as she could escape from the loneliness in the flat.

Chapter Three

She had hesitated a moment between her tight trousers, to-reador-style, which she wore with a blouse when she went to the beach, and a dress with red spots that she had bought a week ago at Galeries Nouvelles, the same shop where Maud had stolen the patent-leather handbag. She had finally chosen the dress. She had made herself look pretty and smart, done her hair nicely, and set off to window-shop on Rue d'Antibes.

During the past days, when the sky had been overcast and it had been cold, Cannes had been nothing but an ordinary, small provincial town. But as soon as the sun began to shine again, it was impossible not to know that you were on the Riviera. The tourists invaded the streets, speaking every possible language, men in shorts, like scoutmasters, revealing hairy calves, and women dressed that way as well, some of them enormously fat, others who even wandered along the sidewalks and into the shops in bathing suits, smelling of sun-tan lotion, which was almost becoming the town's distinctive smell.

Once, when Célita and Marie-Lou were out for a walk, more respectably dressed than most of the other women on the streets, two housewives had nonetheless turned around to look at them, guessing what sort of women they were and making uncomplimentary remarks in voices loud enough for them to hear. It had spoiled Célita's afternoon, but Marie-Lou had only murmured, philosophically:

"Don't take any notice, dear. I don't know why we bother how we dress; they always know what we do to earn our living."

It was true. Just the day before, when the married couple was coming out of church, other people there had realized that she belonged to a different kind of world, though the only one to recognize her as the dancer from the Monico had been the man with gray hair.

She turned down a side street to go to the Croisette, because somebody was eying her too inquisitively. From a distance she recognized Francine, in her blue outfit, on the other side of the street, walking along with a middle-aged man.

Célita knew they would go into a boardinghouse, halfway along the street, where you could hire rooms by the night or even by the hour. Francine went in first, then the man, with his head slightly bowed. When she passed the house, she looked in, saw the gloomy hallway, the frosted-glass door, with which she was all too familiar.

She didn't go there very often, and almost always toward the end of the month, when she hadn't enough money to pay the rent, or, as last week, when she wanted a new dress.

She had never asked Léon for a thing, and he would probably never have given her anything. Yet he knew very well how she obtained the necessary cash, since he was more often than not the middleman when customers wanted to proposition any of the hostesses.

Could he ever become jealous? He hadn't with Florence, in the days when they had both been living in Pigalle, he as a bartender in a low sort of club, she, much younger then, unashamedly picking up men, which she continued doing during his eighteen months in jail.

Nobody here really knew the story behind his conviction. It was mentioned as seldom as possible at the Monico, and then only in whispers. One of the musicians maintained that two rival gangs had had a fight in the bar where Léon was working; one man was killed and another left seriously injured in the street, and Léon, with the rest of them, had been held responsible. Ludo didn't believe this story; he knew a lot about those Corsican and Marseille gangs. He claimed that the present owner of the Monico had always operated on his own, a lone wolf, whom both gangs suspected of being in league with the police.

Whichever it was, Léon had married Florence when he got out of jail, and afterward they had set up the business together, with both the Monico and their flat on Boulevard Carnot in her name, as was nearly always done in such circumstances.

By now Madame Florence had been on the job some years. She was thirty-nine, almost forty. She had become middle-class and respectable, and for some time she had been looking unhealthily fat.

Célita, at thirty-two, felt she herself was already old.

Until yesterday the struggle had been between these two women, and Célita had been confident of victory. She remembered that day, during her first week at the Monico, when the proprietor had called to see her in her bedroom at the Hôtel de la Poste, as he did later with Maud. To begin with, he had seemed to think he was only getting his due, as if it were just a matter of routine.

"I suppose I have to put up with it?" she had said to him calmly as he took off his coat and tie.

"Does it surprise you?"

He had been intrigued and taken aback by her tone of voice.

"I'm not surprised at anything any more."

"What did you expect then?"

"Nothing."

She had drawn the curtains and climbed into bed. The whole time she had stared at the ceiling, her body inert, her face indifferent.

"Are you doing this on purpose?"

"Perhaps."

"Are you always so mild?"

She realized that he was put out, not very pleased with himself.

"What else would you like?"

Later, as he got dressed, he had mumbled:

"You think you've been real smart, I bet."

She had had to hide her little smile of satisfaction, because she knew now that she had chosen the right line, that he was intrigued, humiliated, and that he would come again, determined to bring her to heel.

That evening, all the others, except Natasha, who had not yet arrived in Cannes, heard about his visit.

"Well, did he get what he wanted?"

Marie-Lou, like a good friend, warned her.

"Whatever happens, don't get ideas and imagine that this is it! It's just a craze of his. He's got to feel he's the boss, show he's a real man. You see? He'll probably sleep with you a couple of times, just casually, but it'll be such a trifling affair his wife won't even be jealous. . . ."

It was true. To judge by her attitude, Madame Florence was

going out of her way to show Célita, who was the new girl then, that she knew all about it and took no offense.

"We'll see!" Célita had replied to Marie-Lou, out of sheer bravado.

"See what?"

"Nothing."

Had she thought up her plan then? She couldn't say. More likely it had just come to her little by little. At first, it had been a kind of game. For her, he wasn't Monsieur Léon, or even plain Léon. He was the man. And, beside him, there was Madame Florence, the woman to be ousted.

Célita had not been deaf to the mutterings that went on behind her back, and Marie-Lou, ever incapable of holding her tongue, had been unable to conceal from her what she was thinking.

"You're envious, Célita. If something nice happens to other people, it makes you mad, and you'd do almost anything to stop them from being happy."

This was not quite true. Once, soon after Natasha's arrival, when they were still friends, they had had a long talk on the subject. Natasha was more intelligent than Marie-Lou or Ketty, or the other girls who had spent some time at the Monico. She used to read a lot and was the only one never to go to bed with any customer. Nobody was quite sure if she'd even let the proprietor have her.

She was married to a traveling salesman and had a child, a little girl of three. She had left her husband, and the divorce she had asked for was now being heard. She claimed custody of her daughter, and she expected the court's decision any day now.

"They say I'm envious because I'm different from them."

"Other people hate anyone to be different from them."

"It's not envy with me; it's just that I loathe injustice. . . ."

Natasha had seemed to be sympathetic at that time, and they had nearly shared a flat together on Rue Pasteur.

"Some people have all the luck, and they're always the ones who deserve it least. Look at Marie-Lou, for example; she's as stupid as the backside of a cow, and everyone's nice to her. . . ."

Why had Natasha tired of her? A few days later she had turned cold and deliberately avoided Célita, who had asked her openly:

"Have I done anything wrong?"

"What do you mean, wrong?"

"I don't know. I just wondered why you've changed toward me."

"You tire me."

After a silence, she added, searching for the right words:

"You're too complicated. You try to dramatize yourself all the time. . . ."

Was it her fault if drama seemed to cling to her? Hadn't she always tried to do her best, intensely, passionately?

Natasha should have understood; she knew the story of Célita's past.

"When I was four, I had to sleep with the woman next door—just like Pierrot—on Rue Caulaincourt, while my mother was dancing in nightclubs, and when I was eight, she sent me to a ballet school, where I suffered absolute hell, dancing on my toes and dislocating every part of my body. And all that time I had a brother and sister in Hollywood, being spoiled by their wealthy parents. Do you know who my father is?"

She had told her: José Delgado, the famous singer and movie star, whose picture was often in the papers.

"I was born too soon, when he was a nobody, sharing a room in Montmartre with my mother. He never married her, and left for the United States when I was two. Over there he got married three times, had other children; they say he's getting divorced again, and there'll be yet another wedding. . . ."

"What difference does it make to you?" Natasha had retorted.

She didn't understand, and yet she could not have led a very happy life herself, having left her husband and having to fight for her daughter. As for Marie-Lou, provided she no longer had to be a maid-of-all-work and get up at six o'clock in the morning, all her problems were solved. Now and again she fell in love, which might last for three weeks or a month. The latest was a croupier from the Casino who looked like an undertaker's mute.

At the age of sixteen, Célita had been in the chorus of various operettas touring smaller towns and second-rate casinos, having her meals more often in trains and station snack bars than in proper restaurants.

Nevertheless, she had once had her own man, when she was twenty-two—a man with whom she lived, admittedly in a hotel room on Boulevard Saint-Martin—and made plans for their future together. When she found out she was pregnant, she had imagined he would share her joy. In her third month, she was still dancing at the Châtelet.

Her lover worked for a shipping firm, and she was happy to think she would soon be able to escape from the theater. They would have a little house in the suburbs, more children, a car later on.

Everything seemed settled, when a woman, a sly-looking, small brunette, who wasn't even pretty, took him from her.

"They're married now, Natasha. They're happy. They've got three children going to school. . . ."

"And yours?"

"Mine died. It was a little girl. Since her father had left me, she was all I had."

She paused, wanting some sympathy, at least some sign of approbation.

"Can you imagine what it was like?"

"What happened?"

"I didn't want to board her in the country. I needed to have her near me. In the evenings, like Francine, I let a woman on the same floor look after her for me. Nothing's happened to Francine's little boy. Nothing will happen to him. Nothing awful ever happens to other people. When my baby was thirteen months old, she was suffocated by the woman who was looking after her. She had taken the baby into her own bed because she was crying. She was drunk that evening, I know, because she stank of alcohol the next morning, and she hadn't noticed anything."

"You haven't had much luck, you poor thing."

And Célita flung back:

"It's not a matter of luck; it's a matter of justice!"

She had decided to fend for herself, to fight, if need be. Operettas were almost a thing of the past. The theaters were turning dancers away, or they wanted them young.

"I'm thirty-two. It'll soon be too late. . . ."

She didn't like talking about her experiences of the last ten years.

"Before long they won't even take me as a saleswoman at Prisunic!"

Did Marie-Lou ever worry about the future? Or Ketty? Or Natasha? Were they still hoping to find a husband, at the Monico or elsewhere?

"Nobody's ever bothered their head over me. I'm damned if I'm going to bother about other people!"

Poor Madame Florence, if Célita should succeed!

It was a three-sided struggle, because the first one to deal with was Léon himself. He wanted people to think of him as a real man, and he believed he had had a lot of experience. As far as he was concerned, the girls who came and went at the Monico were worth a visit, sometimes two, after which he couldn't care less. He did it rather as if he were a cattleman branding his herd.

But after six months he had still not been able to leave Célita alone, and he could not have explained how she managed it. She was sometimes convinced that he had guessed where her ambitions lay.

"You know, sweetheart," he had told her during the second week, "it's no use your getting any big ideas. There's nothing doing. Maybe we do go to bed together now and then, but it ends there. There are plenty of others, smarter girls than you, who've tried to get their clutches on me. Just ask my wife . . ."

A month later, staring into her eyes, he was questioning her, furious:

"What have you been planning inside your little head?"

She forced a laugh.

"You're the nastiest, most vicious bitch I've ever come across."

He hated not understanding something and felt humiliated when somebody stood up to him.

"Can you ever have actually been in love with anyone?"

"It would be funny if I was just beginning to learn now. . . ."

Between Madame Florence and Célita, the war was at once pettier and crueler, made up of slight annoyances and smiling treacheries. Some months Célita had collected so many five-hundred-franc fines that at the end she got nothing, and even in front of the customers, the proprietress never hesitated to insult her.

Yet Célita remained, and it was Florence who was frightened. Only two days ago, Léon had spent a couple of hours at Place du Commandant-Maria, and for the first time he had said afterward, just as he was going:

"It would be more convenient if you got rid of Marie-Lou and had the place to yourself. . . ."

Was she imagining things or was he beginning to need her?

But now there was Maud. . . .

And Maud was there, on the beach, lying in the sun near a blue umbrella. Célita was making her way along the Croisette, which, almost overnight, had assumed its summer look. Here, everybody was on holiday, climbing out of cars, walking around taking pictures, or relaxing on the sandy beach, stretched out in their bathing suits.

Did these holiday-makers in their brightly colored clothes, their bodies sunburned to a greater or lesser degree, also have their worries?

At any rate, there was one consolation: Maud was not with Léon in her hotel bedroom, as Célita had feared.

One of them had gone to get her, Ketty or Natasha. They had enrolled her in their little group right away, and she was lying in the spot usually reserved for Célita.

While his mother was at the boardinghouse, Pierrot, his hair gleaming in the sun, was playing under the watchful eyes of the three young women in bikinis, as they chatted among themselves.

Ketty, glancing up, saw Célita first and pointed her out to the others. They must have been talking about her, because Ketty said:

"Careful! There she is. . . ."

They didn't wave to her, pretended not to have noticed her. Like them, Célita was wearing dark glasses, which made her features look hard; she walked more slowly, seemed to hesitate over whether to go down to the sand, then casually sat in one of the deck chairs near the railing, just opposite them.

Pierrot saw her and rushed up to tell Natasha:

"Do you know Célita's up there?"

Natasha must have replied:

"Leave her alone! Don't look her way! We have nothing to do with her."

"Why not?"

"It doesn't matter. Don't worry your head over it."

"Has she been naughty?"

Maud's skin was whiter than the others', and instead of a bikini she was wearing a respectable bathing suit. Pierrot was obviously not satisfied with the replies he had been given, and after staring at Célita for quite a while, screwing up his eyes because of the sun, he turned away regretfully and went to paddle in the water.

The three women, knowing they were being watched, played a little game of pretending to whisper secrets to each other with great glee.

Célita had not spent much time at school, but the same sort of thing had gone on at kindergarten and, later on, before and after dancing lessons, except that the mothers also joined in then and were even nastier than their daughters.

A young married couple was holding hands on a bench close by, watching the sea; perhaps they were seeing it for the first time. Meanwhile, a little farther along, an old man could not take his eyes off a plump woman lying face down on the sand who had unfastened the top part of her bikini.

The second show, the night before, had been less of a triumph for Maud than the first. She had made practically the same gestures, in the same order, but it seemed, this time, as if she didn't have her heart in it, as if she was repeating a lesson she had learned, and just as she was about to uncover her breasts, she had stood there for a moment, lost, as if she had forgotten what was to come next, or as if she had suddenly become aware of the incongruousness of her behavior.

Yet they had applauded her. She had not waited for the proprietor to come to her, but picked up her clothes and hurried through the door with the peephole. A little later Monsieur Léon had gone up to her in the dressing room, probably to tell her not to lose heart.

He would go to see her, as he had gone to see the rest. It would be interesting to see if she could keep him returning for more than a week.

Léon must be very angry with Célita for having called the police. He had steered clear of her all evening and not said good night to her. Perhaps she had been wrong to leave the flat? He might have come to see her this afternoon, to reproach her.

The other three were keeping up their playacting, though with less enthusiasm. Natasha called to Pierrot and gave him a bun she had just bought from a beach vendor.

"Hello, Mademoiselle Célita."

She jumped, even though she recognized Emile's voice. He was wearing blue jeans, a green cotton shirt, and was carrying a bundle of fliers.

"Are you by yourself?"

Before she could answer, he saw the others on the beach.

"I knew it," he said.

"Knew what?"

"That they'd do this to you. They decided last night never to speak to you again and to treat you as if you didn't exist."

He remained standing, one hand resting on the arm of an unoccupied chair.

"Sit down for a moment."

"No thanks. I don't want to disturb you and I'm not looking very sharp. Marie-Lou tried to stick up for you."

"Are you sure she did?"

"Yes. I heard her say: 'It's not really her fault! She gets so unhappy.' "

"Isn't the boss at the Monico?"

"Was it you who phoned just before four? I thought it might be, but Madame Touzelli had already hung up. He's taken Madame Florence to Nice, to see a doctor."

"Is she ill?"

"I don't know. He called a doctor I've never heard of and made an appointment. . . . You won't be angry, Mademoiselle Célita, will you, if I tell you . . ."

He hesitated, abashed, turned toward the sea and went on:

" . . . if I tell you that I'm on your side?"

"You don't think I played a dirty trick?"

"That's not for me to say, is it? I know that as far as you're concerned I don't count, I'm just a kid, and what I think isn't important. . . ."

"What do you think?"

Down on the beach they were nudging each other, staring at the odd couple, Emile and Célita.

"You needn't be frightened! Tell me!" she went on.

"I don't think you're going to get what you're after—with the boss, that is."

"What am I after?"

"Madame Florence's place. Everybody knows that. She too."

"Has she said anything to you about it?"

"I've heard her mention it to her husband."

"What did she say to him?"

"You want me to tell you?"

"Yes."

" 'If you suppose I'll ever let that whore take my place at the desk . . .' "

"Did you believe her?"

He blushed without answering, and there was a slightly awkward silence. But after a while he sighed, then murmured, still hesitating:

"If you ever need me for anything, I'll be there."

"Do you think I ever will?"

"I know the boss. I was fifteen when I came to the club. He thinks he's a tough nut. He doesn't stick his neck out with Ludo though, because Ludo probably knows too much about him. As for Madame Florence, she knows him better than anybody; she gives him a little rope, but she knows he'll always come back to her in the end. . . . Can I ask you one question that's been on my mind?"

"Go ahead."

"Do you love him?"

She looked at him, her eyes hard.

"Tell me you don't love him," he went on, "that he sometimes disgusts you."

"All men disgust me."

"Me too?"

"You're only a child."

"You think that too—I know you do—and you don't see that I'm the only person who loves you. You sleep with the boss. You sleep with other men too. I'm not saying that to make you angry. Some of them have even told me details about it afterward. . . ."

He spoke ardently, in a low voice.

"Why do you keep on treating me like a kid? Listen! Don't look at me like that. What's stopping you from doing with me what you do with other people?"

She could only shrug her shoulders, amazed and angry at the same time.

"Is it such a big thing to ask you? And you see how happy it would make me!"

"Who else have you been asking this sort of thing?"

He smiled, flattered, in spite of himself, and acknowledged:

"Some people don't have to be asked."

"Who?"

"You'd be surprised if you knew."

"Who?" she repeated.

"One of them's pretty near here."

"Ketty?"

"I don't count Ketty; she does it with everybody."

"Natasha?"

He nodded his head, and Célita sat still, musing. It was quite possible, after all. And, thinking about it, she even seemed to understand Natasha's reasons for wanting to seduce Emile.

"I swear it's different with you, Mademoiselle Célita. I only told you about that to prove I wasn't still a kid. I love you. . . ."

She had to smile.

"It's true, honest it is. And if I had a proper job and didn't have military service still to do, I'd marry you like a shot. . . ."

"Thank you."

"Why do you say it like that?"

"No reason, Emile. I really meant thank you."

"Then, is it yes?"

"It's no."

"But why?"

"There's no why about it. Now please leave me alone."

Disconcerted, but unable to give up hope, he stuttered:

"Not even for five minutes?"

"What do you mean?"

"Just for us to be alone somewhere for five minutes . . ."

He couldn't understand why she suddenly got up and walked away without saying a word. She was abandoning her sole ally, leaving him bewildered in the middle of the Croisette, a batch of pink leaflets in his hand.

He had naïvely asked her for five minutes!

She was prepared for what would happen, yet she determined nonetheless to go to Justin's for supper that evening as usual, merely planning her entry a little late so she could be the last to arrive. Francine always had her meals with her little boy, but the four others were there, at the table at the back, and Maud was sitting in the place usually kept for Célita.

When she came in, Justin looked embarrassed.

"They said you weren't coming."

"It doesn't matter, Justin. I'll eat here."

It was Natasha who was directing operations—she felt sure of it—and Maud was obviously uncomfortable that Célita was sitting by herself at a table near the door.

No move was made toward her. To rile her, the four women were endeavoring to carry on an animated conversation, but it was proving difficult, there were many silences, and they looked like amateur actors putting on a play in a village hall.

"So I told the old guy what I thought of him. . . ."

"The one with the little beard?"

"No, the other one, who comes with that woman with all the new dresses and always pretends to go to the toilet in the hope of catching me in the cloakroom . . ."

Ketty interrupted her:

"He tried it on me too. He wanted to make a date."

"I told him I was an artiste, and for the sort of thing he was after I could give him a good address. . . ."

Did she look around at Célita on purpose? Was the glance meant to insinuate something?

"Whose address did you give him?"

"He didn't want it. Anyway, he didn't have time to listen to any more. He'd just seen his wife, through the peephole, coming across the floor, and he dashed off to the lavatory."

"Justin! Is there any strawberry tart?"

"It's all gone, Mademoiselle Natasha. But there's still some *mille-feuilles*."

It was hard to eat without looking at them, hard too to look at them blankly enough, and the meal seemed, to Célita, to last an eternity. Finally, she kept her mind occupied by counting the cigarette butts in the sawdust on the floor below the bar, then the bottles on the shelves.

It was essential to stick it out, not only here, but later, at the Monico, where it would probably be worse. That afternoon on the beach they had had plenty of time to work each other up and plan all manner of spiteful things.

"Justin! Some Brie and coffee, please!"

"Coming, mademoiselle."

A newsboy came in, and she got through the rest of the meal by burying her head in a paper. She left last, as she had intended, which meant she was three minutes late. From the doorway she saw Madame Florence taking the black notebook from the drawer.

"Good evening, Madame Florence."

The proprietress pointed to the alarm clock on the shelf. Célita didn't give her time to speak.

"Yes, I know, five hundred francs."

Ludo, overhearing this, opened his eyes wide; it was the first time he had ever heard anyone speak so cheekily to the proprietress. Madame Florence was about to call Célita back as she pushed open the door into the cloakroom, but in the end she simply made a mark by her name, then, after a moment's hesitation, added another.

It was Saturday, and the people were different; younger on the whole, they turned up earlier. Until half past ten nothing much happened, although the others continued to ignore Célita and exchanged knowing looks, as if something were being hatched among them.

At half past ten the place was three-quarters full and almost everybody was dancing. Célita had been cornered by a dentist from Lille who had come to the Riviera to enjoy himself and was determined to enjoy himself at any cost. To be ready for the cabaret, about which he asked incessant questions, he had chosen a table on the very edge of the floor, and in twenty minutes he had finished his first bottle of champagne.

Unfortunately, he was an avid dancer, and although he had obviously never been taught, he was convinced that his improvisations were irresistible. Every five minutes he went up to Gianini confidentially, and asked him to play one of his favorite tunes.

"One thing about you, you do let me do the leading," he told Célita happily, as he made her perform the most fantastic steps. "I hate women who think it's their job to show a man how to dance. . . ."

He didn't care if he jostled other couples or trod on his partner's toes, or that he almost fell over several times. On the contrary, the more violent the bumps, the gayer he seemed, like somebody driving a Dodg'em car at a fair.

He felt down Célita's thighs and remarked:

"Funny to think I'll soon be seeing you without any clothes on, here on this very floor! How does it make you feel? Do you get excited?"

Still, every so often he had to sit down for a rest and, above all, a drink, and this gave Célita some respite.

It was while she was enjoying one of these respites that certain looks and smiles made her feel that something was going to happen any moment now, but she found it impossible to imagine where the blow would fall. They were all there, almost all of them with a man, except Natasha and the new girl, who were dancing together.

"Let's have another," the dentist said, wiping his lips.

Since Madame Florence was watching her, Célita didn't dare refuse, and she was back on the floor again in the grip of her disheveled partner. Had someone told the band to quicken the rumba rhythm? Gianini had been watching the dentist and probably thought he'd have some fun.

Célita was following him as well as she could, bumped from left and right, and then all at once her leg twisted, for no apparent reason. She was on her knees before she realized that Natasha had danced past with the new girl and had deliberately hooked one of her high heels in such a way as to jerk off Célita's shoe.

Instinctively she tried to retrieve it, but she could not go on squatting among the dancers' legs, and the shoe had already been kicked far away from her.

The dentist, who had no idea what was happening, asked her:

"Have you twisted your ankle?"

"No. It's my shoe. . . ."

Unable to dance with only one shoe, she attempted to leave the floor, but had little success in pushing her way through the throng.

Three times, four times, she bent down to pick up her black suede shoe, now smudged with dust, whenever it came near her, and each time somebody sent it flying out of reach. It had developed into a game, a sort of soccer match, with everybody eventually joining in.

"Excuse me, please."

She shoved several couples aside and made her way, limping, to her table, as people burst out laughing. Can one ever feel sorry for a woman who looks ridiculous?

"How did it happen?" her partner asked her, resignedly following her off the floor.

"It doesn't matter! Don't bother about me."

Maud, who was still dancing with Natasha, was not laughing, nor did she try to kick the suede shoe, which had by now lost a heel. Marie-Lou was the first to drop the game and take her partner over to the bar.

The music stopped. The floor emptied. Among the streamers in the middle lay the pathetic shoe, stared at by everyone until Jules decided to go and pick it up.

"Is this yours, Mademoiselle Célita?"

The question must have been ironical, since she was sitting there with one foot bare.

"I'll try to find the heel for you. It must be under one of the tables."

"Don't worry. Thanks, Jules."

And her idiot dentist asked:

"I hope you've got another pair?"

"Upstairs, yes."

It was better not to try to cross the room until the customers had started dancing again.

"Will you pour me a drink?"

She bravely managed to smile at him over her glass.

"Here's looking at you!"

Chapter Four

Alone in the dressing room, she collapsed onto a stool in front of the mirror and stared at herself, severely, without pity; probably, at that moment, she hated herself as much as the others hated her.

The grotesque incident of the shoe had shaken her more than if it had been something more serious, and if she had had even five thousand francs to her name she would have left the place that very minute.

She had no idea where she would go. She was too old for the Paris clubs. There was a cabaret in Geneva that was a kind of mecca for striptease artistes, where she had already been for two spells, but it was like a factory belt, fifteen girls every night, sometimes more, following one after another in a series of arranged items. Try Nice? Marseille?

Still, what was the point of thinking about it when she didn't even have the train fare? She had never had any money, here less than ever, since as soon as she had her hands on a few francs she went and staked them at the Casino, not at roulette or chemin de fer, because she had no ticket for the gaming room, but at lotto in the big hall.

She would go back there week after week, however much

she lost, as if to try to force her fate into such a position that it would eventually have to play fair and make her win.

And while she was waiting for this to happen one day, she was more or less trapped in Cannes, with no chance of escaping. It was not the first time; she had been in a similar predicament in the past, in Ankara, an odd sort of place, a capital city built out of nothing, right in the middle of the Asia Minor desert.

She had blessed her good luck when she was sent out there by a Porte Saint-Martin agency, with a six-month contract, and never dreamed that the six months would turn out to be two years.

The cabaret had been a shabby place. All around the room were private boxes that could be curtained off. In all her life she had never fought off so many hands. Each day she swore she would put some money aside for the journey back, whatever the cost, but after two years she was still there, toward the end almost resigned to the fact that she would be there forever. This might have happened had it not been for a Belgian diplomat who was returning to Europe with his family and offered her a job of accompanying his children as their governess.

"You mustn't tell my wife where I met you. I'll pretend that you're a schoolmistress who wants to go home."

During the journey he made the most of her, and suggested keeping her with them at their home in Brussels, not very enthusiastically, it is true, because although it would be convenient for him, he was nonetheless terrified his wife would find out about their relationship.

She had those marvelous green eyes that change color according to the weather, like the sea, and her hair was naturally dark auburn—she never had to tint it; and everybody told her with sickening repetition that her chin and her pointed nose reminded them of the young Colette, the Colette of *Claudine à Paris*.

Everybody considered her sexy. Just now, hadn't the dentist on a spree asked her about her act, which he had not yet seen:

"Doesn't it make you excited when you come out in front of everybody naked?"

He didn't know that she never appeared naked. And besides, if he'd had the opportunity to question them all, one after the other, he would have got a shock to learn that the girls at the Monico were less sexy than those on the beach, for example, where Célita often watched women, young girls even, brazenly revealing themselves to all eyes, lying out flat on the warm, fleshlike sand.

Maybe Maud was like that though; unless, as Célita suspected, she was simply putting it on last night.

As far as the others were concerned, men hardly aroused them at all. Marie-Lou, for example, sometimes got stuck on somebody, but more like a teenager, almost like a little girl, and it was usually because, as she naïvely put it, "he's such a sweet person."

Natasha had found she could sleep alone for weeks and months on end since she left her husband, and what had happened with Emile was something strange, an unexpected pleasure she had allowed herself in passing, like trying some new delicacy when traveling.

Francine lived for Pierrot and nobody else; she would have liked more children, provided the father passed out of her life as soon as possible.

Ketty was the exception. She alone was aggressively and

crudely sex-conscious; she spoke about making love in the dirtiest way, like some of the customers they tried to avoid, but Célita suspected that she exaggerated it all to hide the fact that she was frigid.

For Célita, Madame Florence, and probably millions of other women as well, a man didn't mean sex; nor was it—at any rate not entirely—a question of security.

That afternoon Emile had asked her a question that kept running through Célita's head:

"Do you love him?"

He had added, naïvely, like the boy he was:

"Tell me . . . he sometimes disgusts you."

Well no, he didn't. And perhaps, in her own way, Célita was in love with Léon. Because she had chosen to conquer him. Because she had selected him as her adversary.

He was a match for her, in fact, and since he was continually slipping out of her range, he made the contest difficult, and all the more exciting.

Madame Florence had been through it all too, probably, since she had remained faithful to him, working for him while he was in prison, and also now helped him day after day, showing him she was intelligent enough to ignore his weaknesses.

Célita had decided to take him from her, and it was neither dastardly nor treasonable on her part. It was honest warfare.

Was she going to give up the struggle because of a shoe kicked off her foot, because of a ridiculous girls' conspiracy, like a boarding-school plot?

It was not true that she had a spare pair of shoes here, as she had told the dentist. The only shoes she kept at the Monico were some red satin ones, with rhinestones sewn on them, which she wore for her Spanish dances.

Downstairs they probably thought she was sulking, or crying, or getting her things together to leave. She trembled when she heard steps on the iron staircase, but did not glance through the glass pane down by the floor to see who was coming.

When the door opened, she saw Léon's reflection in the mirror. He held a hammer in one hand, the retrieved heel in the other, and without saying anything he looked for the shoe, picked it up, and walked across to the window ledge.

He loved doing odd jobs, particularly difficult ones, and he turned the black suede shoe around and around in his big fingers for a long time before taking some nails from his pocket and setting to work.

The window ledge was unsuitable for what he wanted to do, so he looked around again, finally noticing the stool Célita was sitting on.

Wasn't he paying her this visit to hold out the olive branch? He was absorbed in his task, frowning, biting his tongue, and he turned the stool upside down to mend the shoe on one of its legs, using it like a cobbler's last.

"Hold the toe."

He made several attempts before he was satisfied with the solidity of his handiwork.

"That'll hold for now, but you'd better not dance on it."

She took the shoe from his hands.

"Thanks."

"It's nothing."

At the door he spoke again, without turning around:

"You must admit you asked for it!"

When she came downstairs, shortly after him, Natasha had taken her place at the dentist's table, and he looked at Célita in embarrassment but didn't invite her back. It would not be long before Marie-Lou and Ketty went up to change into their costumes, and as she walked toward the bar and hoisted herself onto a stool, Célita realized that Marie-Lou would not be sleeping at Place du Commandant-Maria that night.

The last Saturday in every month, the "Man from Switzerland," as they called him, not knowing his real name, would sit in a corner by himself, indifferent to what was going on around him; one evening, quite naturally, without realizing how odd his behavior seemed, he had taken a newspaper from his pocket and started reading.

He was a bank manager from Geneva. Each month he came to Cannes to see a rich customer who was ending his days in one of the most beautiful villas on the Riviera, which he never left except in a car, accompanied by his chauffeur and his nurse.

On his first visit to the Monico, the Swiss had watched them one by one and stayed till closing time. He had danced only once, solely to have the opportunity of speaking to Marie-Lou, who, with her innocent ways, inspired more confidence in him than did the others.

"I won't be coming back with you tonight," Marie-Lou had announced to Célita as they were getting dressed to leave. "That man's waiting for me at the corner."

They had been seen walking off toward the Croisette. Marie-Lou came home at seven o'clock the next morning and, since she didn't have her key, had knocked on the door for ages before she could wake Célita.

"I'm sorry, dear. Do you know what he did? He put his

alarm on for six o'clock without telling me, and then informed me that I had to go, and to take care not to let the staff see me. He's staying at the Carlton, in a suite with an enormous drawing room, number 301, I remember. We didn't even go inside together. He was scared of the porter and told me:

" 'Go up to number 301 in ten minutes and don't speak to anybody.'

"He thought I'd be walking up and down the Croisette while I waited. Of course I went and had a chat with Louis, the night porter. . . ."

Since then, the same performance happened every month, and the Swiss had never thought of changing his partner. He was satisfied with Marie-Lou, and, as she herself said, he hated anything unexpected, anything that makes life complicated. He insisted that everything should conform, once and for all, to established rites.

Because he was there this evening, Célita almost changed her plan once again, because the idea of going home alone, particularly tonight, depressed her. She couldn't leave Cannes without money, but nothing obliged her to stick to Léon, nothing prevented her from going for another man.

The person in the gray tweed suit, the one she had called "God the Father," was here again, sitting in the same place as the night before, with his irritating smiling equanimity. She was convinced it was to see her that he came; she obviously fascinated him. Had he witnessed the scene over the shoe?

Why shouldn't she join the battle all over again, with him, starting from scratch?

She leaned over to Ludo, who had just poured her a Scotch: "Do you know who that is?"

He looked in the direction indicated, shook his head.

"I was wondering too. He doesn't come from Cannes, but he's French and drives a big convertible. Last week, when I was doing some extra work at the Yacht Club, he was there, with all the society people."

The man had guessed they were talking about him, and even what they were saying, because, joining in the game, he took a visiting card from his gold-monogrammed wallet, called the bartender, and asked him to give it to Célita.

She read:

COMTE HENRI DE DESPIERRES

There were two addresses, one on the left, the other on the right: on one side, "Château de Despierres, par Périgueux"; on the other, "23 rue François-Ier, Paris."

She walked over and gave him back his card, saying very coldly:

"Thank you."

"May I buy you a drink?"

"Not now. I've just had a Scotch, and I drank some champagne before that. I'll have to go and get ready soon anyway."

"I know the timetable."

She saw Léon, near the door, watching them, and once again she was tempted to drop everything and start over.

"Are you staying on the Riviera long?"

"Until my wife decides she's had enough."

She had already noticed the ring he wore on the third finger of his right hand, as well as the signet ring, on which, she now realized, his coat of arms was engraved.

"Disappointed?" he asked.

"Why?"

"You might have had ideas about me. If things start going wrong one way, it's only natural to try another."

"What do you mean?"

He merely looked in the proprietor's direction.

"Who told you about that?" she insisted.

"Nobody. I've got eyes. You're a strange girl, Célita."

He had seen her name on the pictures out front, but she was nonetheless disconcerted.

"Your friends are upstairs already. I thought you had to go and change. What are you doing tonight? The cancan?"

The whole time, he seemed to be laughing at her, pleasantly, teasing her, as an elder brother might, and that made her angry. She pursed her lips, left him without saying a word, and went up to the dressing room.

The show was starting. Ketty was going onto the floor. Marie-Lou was pulling on her black mesh tights. After hesitating a moment, because she had promised not to speak to Célita, she said quietly:

"This evening, I'm . . ."

"I know, I saw him."

Marie-Lou was not one for complications and now, alone in the dressing room with Célita, she found herself in a more difficult position than the rest of them.

"You know it wasn't me who . . ."

"Don't upset yourself over me!"

"Maud didn't want to either. Even so . . ."

"Ah!"

"I promise you. She felt lost here, in a new place, so she clung to Natasha, or, rather, Natasha got her claws into her, and the kid doesn't dare . . ."

Madame Florence's voice called, from below:

"Marie-Lou!"

"Coming, madame!"

She pulled at her black satin dress, looked at herself one last time in the mirror, and hurried downstairs.

Célita, in her panties and bra, was putting on her stockings when Maud and Natasha arrived in their turn. In the fanlight she watched them come through the cloakroom and saw Natasha's gesture as she pushed the new girl, who hesitated, toward the staircase.

They both knew she was alone upstairs. Did Maud suppose that Célita would make a scene or tear her eyes out like a cat? But quite the opposite was going to happen, for Célita had made up her mind.

She was going to stay. She refused to alter her objectives. Count What's-His-Name downstairs didn't interest her in the slightest, in spite of his tweed suits, his two houses, and the signet ring with his coat of arms.

Natasha was undressing completely, whereas Maud was only bothering to redo her face and change her pants beneath her tucked-up skirt.

Célita, now ready to go down, looked from one to the other of them, and faced the new girl.

"I'm sorry," she said, in a clear voice that did not tremble, or ask for favors. "I know when I'm in the wrong and I realize I played a mean trick. I've been made to pay for it. I don't bear a grudge against anybody."

No one could have told what was going on underneath this. Abashed, Maud Leroy sought for an answer and, after glancing at Natasha, she mumbled:

"I don't bear you any grudge either, mademoiselle."

She hadn't got used yet to their customary informality.

"You may as well shake hands now," Natasha interposed. "There's no point in going on hurting each other."

Maud's hand was soft, the tips of her fingers rough, like the hands of women who do a lot of sewing.

Natasha went on, still naked, holding her G-string in her hand:

"It was I who found the heel of your shoe and gave it to the boss. As for the dentist downstairs, nothing would please me better than if you'd have him back. In any case, he'll be so tight after the show they'll probably have to cart him out to a taxi."

As Célita was going downstairs, Natasha called her back:

"Aren't you going to shake hands with me too?"

"If you want to . . ."

It was not peace, but an armistice. Or, to Célita's way of thinking, it was undisputedly war, this time. Léon had put himself out to come and mend her shoe, seeming to attach no importance to it, precisely because it was important.

She had sized up the new girl. He would go back to Maud once, twice, perhaps more often. She had youth on her side. But might not her mere nineteen years prevent her from understanding what he wanted?

Florence understood, so did Célita. Because both of them were real women. Like all males, Léon had the urge to dominate, to convince himself that he was achieving a victory, that he was reducing a female to begging for mercy.

That was what he was looking for when he made love in such a brutal, almost vicious way, a cruel flame shining in his eyes.

Célita was ready to struggle with him, a kind of endless struggle, in which she was never absolutely vanquished and the man continually had to prove his prowess.

"You're a little bitch!" he often told her, at the very moment when he should have been most satisfied with her.

He would ask her questions, staring into her eyes, their teeth almost touching.

"You do it on purpose, don't you? Tell me you do it on purpose!"

She said yes, to goad him.

"Do you hate me?" he asked.

"I'm not sure."

This was true, since she had joined in the game herself finally. He was the male. He was the enemy. Whatever happened, she had to win.

It was no longer a matter of security as far as she was concerned, and she wasn't holding on to him simply because she was scared of the Prisunic or the sidewalk that might lie in wait for her.

Life had done its best to drown her; each time she had got her head above water, at the price of a terrible effort, somebody or something had been there to push her under again.

It was for her own sake, for the image she had formed of herself, that it was absolutely necessary to win this particular game.

She hadn't enough time left to take part in many more. On each occasion, the odds grew longer against her. She had been putting all she had into this one for six months, all her ardor, all her determination.

Florence was also playing her last card, even more desperately, since she was nearly forty and was falling ill.

Each was defending what she considered her own property. Neither was asking for any pity.

The position was clear, was it not?

A while ago Célita had almost given in, just over a shoe, because she had felt humiliated. She wouldn't have left, since that was impossible, but she had envisaged throwing herself at that lousy God the Father, who was a count into the bargain.

She felt angry with herself now for having been able to think of it, even for a moment.

Maud had shaken her by the hand. Her skin was pale, there were needle pricks at the tips of her fingers, and one felt something about her body to be unfinished or not quite healthy. In a few minutes she would be walking out onto the floor again, white with fear, gluing her eyes on Gianini, who supported her with his music as effectively as if he were holding her by the shoulders.

Perhaps she was not quite so innocent as she appeared? She had been able to make her decision all by herself, at Bergerac, and she had set off into the unknown with hardly enough to live on for a week. She had paid the price at Marseille, sleeping with a barkeeper whom even Léon seemed to consider a brute. She had not hesitated to steal a handbag and, later, for the inspector's benefit, she had known how to burst into tears in the most touching way.

As for the striptease part of it, which kept everybody breathless, Célita was becoming more and more convinced that it was a fake.

But she had made a mistake to get involved in the fight, to climb into the ring, as it were, to come between Célita and Madame Florence.

She was the wrong weight.

"And now, ladies and gentlemen, we have pleasure in introducing to you Mademoiselle Célita, the famous Spanish dancer, who has been acclaimed in the leading cabarets of Europe. . . ."

Her face at the peephole, she smiled sarcastically. Marie-Lou brushed past her, hurried toward the staircase, leaving behind a strong smell of sweat.

In five minutes everyone would know that Célita had sued for peace.

That evening there was another skirmish, but one of a different sort. Just before, as if to prove Natasha's point, the dentist, who had been giving a solo performance on the dance floor, wearing a cardboard cowboy hat, had suddenly collapsed while hanging on to a table, which had overturned, together with the bucket, the bottle of champagne, and the glasses.

The proprietor had helped Ludo to get rid of him, Jules had tidied up the mess, and the band had struck up a rumba, while Maud, who had received as much applause as on the night before, went and sat by herself in the corner, still the same shy little girl.

Célita had deliberately not rejoined the count. She saw him pay for his drinks, then, instead of collecting his things from the cloakroom, walk over and sit down beside the new girl.

Maud was obviously still observing the rules of the game, or at least pretending to observe them, because, knowing Célita had previously been with her new escort, she turned toward her with a questioning look, as if asking her permission.

"Go ahead, girl!"

At least that was the meaning behind Célita's dumb show.

Strange to say, it was the proprietor who seemed displeased, or worried. Was he afraid Maud might be taken from him even before he had had time to make the most of her?

Marie-Lou, who had just learned of the reconciliation, passed close to Célita, and whispered to her, touching her shoulder:

"You did the right thing!"

"Thanks!"

She probably thought her advice had borne fruit. Poor fat fool!

Somebody asked her to dance just as a large party entered, four couples in a group, probably straight from the gala night at the Casino, since they were in evening dress. Tables were pushed together to make room for them.

The count was not dancing. Leaning toward Maud, he was talking to her seriously, as if he were proffering her the advice of an older and more experienced man of the world. Had he shown her his visiting card yet?

During a break between dances, as Célita was having a drink at the bar, Ludo said to her:

"I saw the name on the card. I know him now. I'd heard about him, but I didn't know this was the one. He married an American twenty years older than him, and she makes his life miserable."

It was now Célita's turn to put on a God the Father smile as she looked over at Maud's companion.

"You prostitute!" she couldn't help muttering to herself.

To think that she had almost taken him on!

She looked around for Léon and found him in conversation with a regular visitor, a shopkeeper from Rue d'Antibes who came to the Monico only when his wife was staying with her mother in Grenoble. The proprietor gave Célita a wink across the crowded room, as if to say to her:

"Well done, my girl!"

He had heard that she had made her apology, but he was far from suspecting the reasons that had prompted her to do so.

It was a long evening, an exhausting one, mainly on account of the party in evening dress, who, as well as champagne, had ordered caviar. All the girls except Maud, who had only one possible number, were obliged to dance twice.

The party looked as though they would never get tired, and even at four o'clock there was no telling when they would go.

Léon still kept his eye on Maud and the count. At one stage, when the latter went off to the lavatory, the proprietor made a point of being in the cloakroom, in order to waylay him.

Naturally enough, he didn't make a scene. Célita could see him through the peephole, jovial, but embarrassed.

She could almost swear he would be saying something of this kind:

"That girl's not like the rest, you know. . . . I'd be careful, if I were you. . . ."

He was to stake his claim to her before anyone else stole a march on him. Who knows but he might not presently send his wife off home by herself while he saw Maud back to the Hôtel de la Poste.

"Idiot!"

He reminded her of Emile, who, trembling, begged her for five minutes as if his life depended on it.

The Man from Switzerland was getting impatient. Marie-Lou had asked Madame Florence if she might leave before closing time, but to no avail. Upstairs there was a typewritten notice next to the mirror giving the House Rules, which dealt with every possible contingency, particularly stating that the artistes were required to stay until 4:00 A.M. at least, and never to leave until the last customer had gone. It also covered things like fines and personal hygiene, and prohibited "throwing cotton balls etc. down the toilet."

Two hours ago, Célita had considered the idea of escaping from this tiny world in which chance had deposited her.

She was finding herself, instead, more deeply involved than ever, but she was going to face it with defiance.

She could no longer risk defeat.

They did not always bother to change in the morning before they returned home. Especially when it was very late, they often went off in the dresses they wore between shows, and carried, over their arms, the clothes in which they had come.

Closing time was like the end of classes at school. The musicians could be seen putting their instruments away in their cases, Jules and the bartender went around collecting glasses and empty bottles, while Madame Florence made up little bundles of francs and slipped them into a big yellow envelope, which she took away in a handbag almost as big as a cabinet minister's portfolio.

Léon saw to the lights, sniffing in the corners, treading on cigarette butts because he was haunted by fear of a fire. He was always the last to leave, locking the door before joining his wife in their car.

They said good-bye more or less as opportunity arose. Everyone had, as it were, to fend for himself.

"Are you going to Justin's?"

"No. I'm not hungry."

"I could do with some spaghetti. . . ."

Marie-Lou met her Man from Switzerland at the street corner, and they went off arm in arm toward the Carlton like a regular couple. They could hear the sound of the sea, saw it becoming paler with approaching day. In the harbor some fishermen were starting the engine on their boat, and at the Forville market the farmers' wives were setting out their baskets and crates, while Justin busily served coffee and white wine.

Célita had not seen the count leaving. Maud had remained until the end, and there was just a chance that the proprietor might have accompanied her home.

She was walking alone, careful not to twist the heel that had been mended. Just as she was taking the shortcut, by the bridge over the railway, she heard steps behind her.

She was always frightened at nighttime, and, although the sky had begun to turn pale, it was still dark. Without turning around, she walked more quickly, her ears alert, sensing that the unknown person behind her had also quickened his pace.

She was about to break into a run, her key already in her hand, so that she could get inside the door as quickly as possible, when a voice called:

"Célita!"

She stopped still, murmuring:

"Idiot!"

For it was Emile's voice. He had stayed to change in the cloakroom and was wearing his blue jeans and a sports shirt, and must have been shivering in them.

He ran the few yards still separating them while she waited for him.

"What is it?"

"Nothing . . . I saw Marie-Lou with her Man from Switzerland, and I thought you'd be going home alone."

They walked along side by side, and Emile skipped now and then, as he did when he was nipping from car to car to put his fliers behind the windshield wipers.

"I thought you were going back to Le Cannet on your bike. . . ."

His father had been killed during the war and he lived at Le Cannet with his mother, who was a charwoman.

"I don't have to," he said, without further explanation.

One didn't have to be very smart, after his avowals that afternoon, to guess what he was hoping for, and Célita wondered what she was going to do. She wasn't the maternal type, like Marie-Lou, for example, who, though only twenty-five, treated all men, including her pompous banker, like overgrown babies.

Nor was she avid for experience, like Natasha, for whom the boy had been a sort of delicacy to enjoy between meals.

She found herself in an awkward situation, since she didn't want to hurt Emile's feelings and at the same time felt a little scared of him. At the Monico, although he was right on the bottom rung of the ladder, for that very reason people were careless when he was around; he noticed everything, heard everything, and was the only one to go to Florence and Léon's flat sometimes.

Was he already convinced he would attain his object? At any rate, he wasn't talking about it.

"I hear you've been very nice, Mademoiselle Célita."

"Who told you that?"

"Everyone. I was glad, and I knew you would from the start. I even had a bet with Ludo."

"You bet him I'd apologize?"

"I bet him you wouldn't have things in for them. You're different from the rest. Natasha's the one who planned the whole thing. You'd better watch her. The others aren't intelligent enough to be nasty. By the way, I found out about the doctor at Nice. It's Madame Florence who's ill."

"How do you know?"

"Because he's a specialist in women's diseases."

"A gynecologist?"

"That's the word, yes. I saw it in the telephone book but I couldn't remember it."

They came in sight of the square, where the greengrocer was taking down the shutters of her shop, and an Arab was sitting on a bench, asleep, his head resting on his bent arms. Francine's light was on.

"You left the window open when you came out," Emile remarked.

He was right. When she had left the flat, Célita had not been in the mood to think about shutting windows.

"You shouldn't do that, not on the ground floor. You never know who might have climbed in."

She looked at him, trying hard not to laugh, for she saw through his little game.

"You're afraid for me, I suppose?"

"What if that fellow on the bench had decided to have a sleep inside, or to burgle the place . . ."

"But he didn't, did he?"

"He's not the only one."

"And you think you'd better come in and make sure?"

A moment before, he was smiling too, as if enjoying jug-
gling with his little speeches. But now that she had her foot
on the doorstep, Emile's face suddenly clouded over. He was
so upset he looked as if he would burst into sobs.

"Please, Mademoiselle Célita, I implore you . . ."

She wanted to say no, but she could not bring herself to
do so. Not long ago, Léon had looked at Maud with almost
the same imploring expression and now she would have sworn
that he had not had the patience to wait until the next day,
that he had gone to the Hôtel de la Poste even it if did mean
a row with Madame Florence.

She stayed there, hesitating, her hand holding the key she
had already inserted in the lock.

"I'll leave as soon as you say. . . . And if . . ."

He was loath to make this promise, but finally decided it
was better than nothing at all.

"And if you don't want me to, I won't touch you."

She opened the door, pushed the light button, and left the
door open behind her. He closed it, and she turned right in
the hall, feeling him trembling all over behind her.

With the second key, she opened the door of the flat, re-
membering how untidy she had left it, with the beds unmade.

She realized, bitterly, that it was too late to go back on her
decision.

"Poor Emile," she said, turning on the lights. "I think you'll
be disappointed; you see how women live when they're left
to themselves."

A kind of fury stirred in her breast, and she shoved open
the bathroom door, to reveal the unemptied bath, the towels
lying on the floor.

"Look . . ."

She switched on the light in the kitchen; the breakfast things had not been cleared from the table and the cups had dregs of coffee at the bottom.

"And here . . ."

The two unmade beds, the rumpled sheets, the grayish pillows at one end with traces of lipstick on them, and underwear soaking in the basin . . .

"You still want to stay?"

She threw her coat over a chair, kicked off her shoes, and, as she stroked her bruised foot, the poor booby declared, as if he were reciting the Hail Mary:

"I love you!"

Chapter Five

At the beginning of the evening, they were all misled into thinking things were all right again, including Célita, except perhaps that Célita did not dare to be hopeful too soon, being used to fate going against her. She had been to Justin's with Marie-Lou, and they had found Natasha and Ketty already sitting down to eat. Since there were only two empty places at the table, Célita had paused for a moment, imagining that one of the two places was for Maud.

"I don't think she'll be coming," Natasha said to her. "That's why I told them to set only four places."

Something had happened; you could see from the excited look on their faces. Natasha continued:

"I called her hotel twice, and both times they told me she was out. I stopped there on my way here. The proprietress told me Maud went out at lunchtime, without leaving a message, or having any breakfast, and she hasn't been back."

At half past nine the four of them trooped into the Monico, almost like a line of schoolgirls, and each of them said good evening to Madame Florence. Célita thought she was looking drawn. At twenty-five to ten, as they sat in the dressing room getting ready, Marie-Lou looked at her watch and murmured:

"Five hundred francs!"

A little later they were downstairs, at separate tables; they were told to do this in order to make the room seem "furnished." Madame Florence's eyes had dark rings under them and she had that anxious look of people who appear to be expecting an agonizing pain at any moment. Célita remembered her visit to the gynecologist at Nice.

For a moment she had imagined that the proprietress might perhaps be pregnant, but it was unlikely to happen now, at forty, for the first time.

It must be some disease of the womb, since she had consulted a specialist. Half the women Célita had met had had some kind of operation, usually the removal of one ovary, sometimes both, and it frightened her; the word "womb" conjured up something mysterious to her, something almost sinister, and the thing she feared most in all the world was to see herself, one day, with a violet scar on her stomach.

Monsieur Léon, standing at the door, must have been aware of Maud's absence. He must also have noticed the looks the women were exchanging from each corner of the room, and twice he went through the curtain to stand with Emile on the sidewalk outside.

Quarter to ten . . . Ten to ten . . . Across the room, Marie-Lou mouthed the words:

"A thousand francs!"

Célita had noticed that the proprietor had shaved with more care than usual, that there was still some talcum powder near his ear, and that he was wearing a loud tie she had not seen before. Had he not looked worried, and if Maud had been there, she would have known for certain that he had gone to see her and got what he was after.

She was far from the truth, as she wasn't long in realizing.

A couple had just come in, regular customers who always chose a place near the band. They were a husband and wife who, although only in their middle fifties, had nonetheless been nicknamed "Philemon and Baucis," since throughout the evening they would be holding hands, smiling at the show, smiling at each other, saying only a few words from time to time, like a very old married couple who knew they always thought the same thoughts.

Gianini was playing an old-fashioned waltz for them, popular thirty years ago, which they had requested the first time they had come and which must have brought happy memories back to them.

Léon went up to the cash register, leaned over to whisper something to his wife. His face was more flushed than usual, as if he had caught a touch of the sun. Madame Florence shrugged her shoulders, with a resigned air, and he hurried outside like a man with a mission to accomplish.

Indeed he did have one. Célita would get all the details later, bit by bit, from Emile, or from Ludo, who could hear from his place what they were saying at the cash register.

The Hôtel de la Poste was a few yards away, on the same street, and that was where Léon was running.

When he came back a quarter of an hour later, he was alone, but his face was lit up, and he was obviously finding it difficult not to look triumphant as he told his wife what had happened.

Maud had not arrived on time because she had gone to sleep after coming back from the islands, at seven that evening, and there had been nobody to wake her.

"Poor child!" Célita had sneered, when, having gone outside for a moment, against the rules, she heard the whole story from Emile.

The proprietor was behaving so much like a lovesick suitor it was embarrassing. It was out of character for him to lose control like this, and everyone had noticed his loud tie and the boyish, almost frisky manner he had unintentionally adopted.

Did he realize he was making a fool of himself? He thought he'd put his "mark" on the new girl, to use his phrase, but in fact it was she who had put her mark so oddly on him.

He stood there waiting for her impatiently, moved by the fact that he had found her asleep, unaware of the time, just like a child. Had they both caught a touch of the sun?

The event had not taken place in the drab hotel bedroom—that would not have been romantic enough. They had gone by boat to the Iles de Lérins, like a honeymoon couple, and no doubt Maud had romantically let her hand trail in the water.

Had they climbed the uneven steps to the fortress, hand in hand, and visited the cell of the Man in the Iron Mask? Had they been to see the monks at Saint-Honorat afterward?

Célita and Madame Florence, probably occupied with the same thoughts, did not dare look at each other now; they were ashamed for him. Long past Emile's age, he just looked ridiculous.

The silly ass was looking at his watch every few minutes, not noticing that even the members of the band were exchanging winks.

Ketty was dealing with four new customers, and Natasha and Marie-Lou were dancing together, when the new girl, wearing the same little black dress, half-opened the curtains at the entrance with the hesitating, timid look of a mouse.

She went right up to Madame Florence. Célita could not hear what she was saying, but she saw the proprietress's cold, resigned face as she dryly accepted the explanation—what else could she do?—and directed her to her place at the front of the room.

Célita had underestimated the girl from Bergerac; she realized that now. Maud Leroy had chosen the fragile approach: the poor little thing who is scared of life and needs a man's support.

And Léon, despite his experience, had fallen for it! Even his walk had changed, had become lighter, more youthful. It seemed that he might start jumping over chairs, as people sometimes do when leaving a cinema, imagining themselves the hero of a film.

He avoided catching Célita's eye, or his wife's. Had the latter already been warned of his new plan, which he was about to see realized?

A reporter from the *Nice-Matin*, Julien Bia, who sometimes stopped at the Monico for a drink, came in, and this evening he had his camera with him. It was obvious that it had been arranged for him to come, that Léon had either seen him or telephoned him.

Sure enough, the proprietor rushed up to him, led him off to Maud's table, called to Jules to bring a bottle of champagne and three glasses.

He was determined to launch the girl, to make her into a star, and the reporter, who had interviewed most of the visiting celebrities along the Riviera, nonetheless gravely took a pen and pad from his pocket and dutifully prepared to take notes.

He asked her questions as if she were somebody really important, jotted down her answers, and the little slut played her role so well that Célita had a furious desire to walk over and slap her face.

Her sweet-little-girl look was too good to be true, shy and sulky at the same time. Trust Léon, the former pimp, not to have made the mistake of buying her a new dress and giving her a hairdo and a manicure!

She was quite capable of having thought of that herself. So she managed to appear to be someone you might meet in the street or behind a counter, or, even more, a young girl who has just stepped off an all-night train, slightly rumpled, tired-looking, holding a cheap suitcase, and you don't know where she's come from or where she's going.

Nor would she have changed her underclothes or her stockings; she was too clever for that. Her cheap little panties, like those worn by typists and chambermaids, stimulated men's imagination and gave them a stronger impression of feminine mystery than the mesh tights, black wasp waists, and spangled G-strings the professionals wore.

What could she be telling the reporter in her artless way, as if her adventure was the most ordinary thing in the world, as if all the small-town girls of France were leaving home to start taking their clothes off in nightclubs the very next day?

It would be in the paper tomorrow. Not everything, since more than fifteen minutes had gone by—enough time for the reporter to fill two columns with her story—before he put his pen and pad in his pocket.

He got up and stepped backward to take photographs, while Léon modestly moved away a little, and Madame Florence turned her head.

Julien Bia was not leaving yet. He waited until Maud's number was over, because he also had to have some shots of the girl in action. He even took one of her almost naked as she leaned over backward on the floor in a sort of spasm, but this one would certainly never appear in the newspaper. It was for Léon!

Gianini had changed his patter, and it was obviously not he who had composed the new formula.

"And now, ladies and gentlemen, the management of the Monico has the honor and the pleasure of presenting to you the great discovery of the year, the artiste who will be tomorrow's unrivaled queen of striptease, Mademoiselle Maud Le Roy, nineteen years old, who has astounded, and will continue to astound, everyone who has seen her. . . ."

The management had the *honor* . . .

The name Leroy had been split into two words, and it would appear that way in the paper the next morning, not only in the account of the interview, but in the large advertisements that would announce Maud to the public in letters four times the size of those used for the other dancers.

In addition, outside the club and on walls around town, a band would be pasted across the old notices until new ones were ready:

MADEMOISELLE MAUD LE ROY
The year's most exciting sensation!

Célita and Madame Florence were not the only ones to have realized all this. As the evening wore on, the others also became glummer, as if the new girl had taken something away from them.

The atmosphere was different. Granted, whenever a new artiste arrived, there had always been a certain tense curiosity, and, in a way, they formed common cause against the stranger as they waited to see whether she would last, and whether she would prove friendly or not.

Nor was it the first time the proprietor had taken a personal interest in a dancer. But at least he had remained himself, and more often than not it had been the girl who won sympathy.

This time a new element had entered the Monico, and Célita had been alone in sensing the danger right from the first day.

"It's time, Marie-Lou. . . . Tell Ketty . . ."

"Yes, madame."

Madame Florence seemed not so bad-tempered, not so much the proprietress, and all at once they wanted to be nice to her.

Occasionally, Léon had to sit with some of the customers, or buy a policeman or a reporter a drink or a bottle of wine. But he had never been known to remain sitting there like this, for two hours, indifferent to the thousand details on which he normally kept an eye.

Contrary to what might have been expected, they hardly mentioned it when they were upstairs changing, or when they passed each other on the iron staircase or in the cloakroom. Nor did they exchange the facile little jokes the situation might have provoked.

It was as though an illness weighed upon them all, perhaps because they knew that the situation was out of their control. There was also a degree of embarrassment added to their natural uneasiness.

Would one of them be kicked out now that there was another permanent number in the show? Ketty was the least successful performer; she was usually sent on first, when people were not quite settled. But Ketty had been there the longest. As a hostess, she had more energy than the others. And, though it was never mentioned, she was ready to follow any customer back to his hotel after the show, or to arrange to meet him the next day.

Was Marie-Lou perhaps in a more dangerous position, since it was impossible to get her to wash herself properly and send her clothes to be cleaned, in spite of fines and Madame Florence's continued admonitions?

Her good temper stood in her favor; she was the only one who never had her bad days, and she coped equally well with rowdy drunks and the kind of customer who wanted to tell his life story.

Natasha's sculptural nakedness was the photograph in the glass case outside that attracted the most people. And up until now, Célita's had been the "prestige" number; she was a real dancer, the only one. In other words, the Monico was not a vulgar dive where one went only to watch girls undressing; it was an artistic cabaret.

"I'll be the one!" she announced to Marie-Lou, whom she found deep in thought by the cloakroom door.

They were obviously all preoccupied by the same subject, for Marie-Lou simply replied:

"More likely me!"

They had been sharing a secret all day. Marie-Lou had come home early, because her Swiss friend, scared of the hotel staff as usual, had made her get up at six o'clock. She had spent a good ten minutes in the bathroom before going to bed. Since she had had three abortions, and the last had almost killed her, she now took double precautions.

Célita had vaguely heard her getting into bed; then, later, the alarm had sounded, Marie-Lou had gone to make the coffee, and when she had set the table and there was a semblance of order in the living room, she had come and pulled off the sheet Célita had twisted around herself.

"Get up, lazybones!" she had called, good-humoredly, although normally she would never open her mouth before she had drunk her coffee.

Célita had finally opened her eyes, and had then realized what had happened. Marie-Lou, with her floral wrap open, revealing her big breasts and the black triangle below her stomach, was wearing Emile's cap on her head.

"Well, my little slut! . . ."

What could Célita say? She didn't regret what she had done. In all her life she had never seen a person's face show such happiness as Emile's had last night. On leaving, he had awkwardly kissed her hands and mumbled:

"Thank you! I'm sorry."

"Sorry about what?"

Then he said something she had not expected, which she was to recall many times:

"For being only me!"

He was a good boy! That evening, when she entered the Monico with the others, he had had the tact, so uncommon in men, not to stare at her in any special way, but to act as if nothing had happened between them.

Marie-Lou had been nice about it too, in the end. She had not teased her too much. And almost immediately she had become serious and promised:

"Don't worry. I won't breathe a word."

She had told Célita how she had made love with the boy one afternoon, almost by accident, when she had gone to the Monico to get her dress, and the proprietor had been out. They had done it in the cloakroom, among the bottles and party hats, while the two old women were sweeping up the paper streamers on the other side of the peephole.

Marie-Lou knew that it meant more to Célita than it had to her. She had at least one quality: humility. She placed herself on the bottommost rung of the ladder, seeing herself as a household drudge who had preferred to earn her living by taking off her clothes in public than by drying dishes and washing floors.

Natasha impressed her because she read serious books and because you could tell she'd had some education. In her eyes, Célita was even better. She not only had a famous father, but she was a real dancer, who had appeared in big theaters in Paris.

Ketty came of peasant stock too and had spent her youth in a poverty-stricken village in Savoy. But, as she was so fond of asserting, she was an egalitarian, and no one could impress her, neither the rich nor the well-educated, although she did have an unconscious passion for doctors, perhaps because she contrasted them with priests, for whom her Catholic childhood had left her with nothing but hatred.

It was half past twelve when the reporter left, escorted right to the door by the proprietor, who stayed a few minutes longer with him on the sidewalk outside. When Léon came back, he went straight over to the cash register, a little ashamed to have to go and explain things to his wife. He had hardly begun talking to her when he was frowning at the sight of an American officer in mufti sitting at Maud's table and engaging her in conversation.

Through Ludo, Célita later learned what Léon had said to Madame Florence:

"Julien Bia is of my opinion. He thinks she's terrific and says I should sign her up, with a long contract."

Madame Florence had replied:

"Most of them are terrific the first few days."

That was true. More precisely, it was either all or nothing. They were either flops, overcome by panic, or their very shyness, the excitement they felt as they faced the public, communicated itself to the audience and won the day for them.

It wasn't till later, when they tried to perfect a proper number, that difficulties began, and so few of them were able to surmount them that cabaret proprietors were always having trouble reinvigorating their programs.

But how could Léon, especially after the excursion to the islands, be anything but optimistic?

"She's caught on. She's a much more intelligent girl than I thought. Her nervousness is deceptive. You know what she said to Bia?

" 'You've got to try to make the spectators feel they're surprising a woman in her bedroom, not watching an artiste do an act.'

"She added:

" 'Since I'm no artiste, and haven't any experience, it won't be difficult for me.'

" 'Unless you find you can't help getting experienced,' our friend Bia retorted, the wise guy.

"And she said:

" 'I'll take care to stay just as I am, not to change my way of life or my ideas.' "

It was half past one when Ludo reported this conversation to Célita, and the proprietress, who had been feeling, or pretending to feel, unwell all evening, had gone home to bed, a rare thing for her, and left the cabaret in her husband's care.

Célita had wondered whether this was a strategic withdrawal, a rather naïve way of making an impression on Léon. Yet it was true that Madame Florence had not been in good health for some time, and she had consulted a gynecologist.

The Maud affair had gone further than they could have foreseen, and it was impossible, as yet, to say which of them, she or Léon, had had the idea that showed near-genius.

This too emerged from the conversation between Léon and his wife immediately after the departure of the reporter. For Maud had said to Bia:

"I'll take care to stay just as I am, not to change my way of life or my ideas."

He had objected, looking around rather ironically:

"You'll have a hard job if you spend all your evenings here."

And, raising his glass:

"Especially if you start drinking champagne and whisky with the customers!"

Was it not a stroke of genius on Maud's part to have answered:

"That's exactly why I'm going to ask Madame Florence not to let that happen to me. It's in her interest as well as mine. Sitting here at a table or at the bar, I'm no use; I'm not a hostess. And if the customers see me here doing that sort of job, they'll stop believing in my act. Don't you see? I must stay looking like the girl next door."

She must have slid the proprietor a conspiratorial glance as she said this. If it was she who had thought up the idea, she was formidable.

How could the fool's conceit of himself as a potent male fail to be flattered by her wanting to keep out of other men's hands? What exactly had passed between them on the islands? Célita was tempted to believe nothing had happened at all.

Maud had probably pretended to be the poor little girl whose two experiences of sex—no, three; there was the Marseille episode—had left her wounded, feeling unclean, needing time to forget, needing patience, tenderness.

"Smart work!" Célita couldn't help saying to Ludo.

"You smelled a rat from the start! I'm beginning to wonder if it might not have been better for all concerned if Inspector Moselli had hauled her off the first night."

"What did Madame Florence reply?"

"They've made no decision yet. She did her bit. Besides, that's when she mentioned the pains in her stomach and announced that she didn't think she'd be able to last until closing time."

That was quite smart work too, since there are occasions when one should know how to beat a retreat. That evening she was an obstacle, sitting there at the cash register, and her husband couldn't help feeling that she was spying on him—and hating her for it. Don't men need to imagine that they are free?

Her indisposition, whatever it was, came just in time, and after the second show Maud did not return to sit at her table. She descended the iron staircase wearing her hat and carrying her handbag, like a visitor, and Léon escorted her to the door and then out onto the sidewalk.

He did not, however, go into her hotel, but returned right away, looking worried, and went behind the bar, where he unhooked the telephone receiver to call his flat.

"Is that you?" he asked in a low voice. "How are you feeling? . . . Have you switched on the electric pad? . . . Nothing special here, no . . . Wait a minute . . . there are still . . ."

His eyes swept the room.

" . . . still about twenty customers. We'll be shutting early. . . ."

She asked no questions about Maud, and it was he who felt it necessary to add, as if reassuring her:

"I've sent the little one home to bed. She could hardly stand up."

"A double Scotch, Ludo," Célita called out loudly.

"Do you think you should, mademoiselle?"

She nodded her head. She felt miserable. It was not so much sadness, as discouragement, sickness at heart. It made her furious to watch a man like Léon, who thought himself a real male, whom she had taken for a real male, get in such a state over a little go-getter.

Once again, she felt she was not being treated fairly.

The way Léon was behaving today was the way she would have wanted him to behave—though a little differently, with more dignity—over *her*.

She knew she was a real woman, a real female to match him, and he would never have made a fool of himself by falling in love with her, as he had now with Maud, almost to the point of losing all perspective, all self-respect.

It was part of the game. It was to be expected. They would have made—they had already begun to make—a fine couple, passionate, tearing away from each other only to come together more completely, shattering one another's pride, humbling each other.

He had understood her so well that he had occasionally felt frightened of her, frightened of being dragged down into the abyss where she was making him want to remain engulfed with her.

Had Célita's hatred of Madame Florence become less bitter?

She knew this was not so. She was sure of herself. She had needed only a little more time to detach him from a tiresome aging woman.

What could be wrong in that? They were wild beasts, the three of them, and wild beasts make their own laws.

"Let the best one win!" is the sporting phrase.

She was convinced she was the best.

He had never looked such a numbskull as he had that evening, with his air of sudden rejuvenation and embarrassment at his happiness. He didn't know what to do with himself, where to look. Deep down, though, he missed his wife, or, rather, her reassuring presence at the cash register.

He couldn't fail to notice that everyone at the Monico, the entire staff, was glancing at him furtively, then exchanging woebegone looks with the others, including Jules, the bald waiter with the watery eyes of a spaniel.

"I'm fed up, Ludo!" she declared, emptying her glass.

"Take a sleeping pill as soon as you get home, and you'll feel better tomorrow."

She looked the proprietor up and down, and said sarcastically:

"Tomorrow? You think so?"

Léon heard her order another double Scotch, knowing very well that she had just finished one and had had several drinks with customers. Would he say something to her, to stop her, or would he tell Ludo not to serve her any more?

She looked straight at him, on purpose, trying to provoke some sort of reaction, even a public showdown, here and now, right away. She felt ready to explode.

He preferred to pretend he had noticed nothing, to push

open the door to the cloakroom and come back with some paper hats, which it was unusual to distribute so late, since the customers no longer needed them.

"See that?"

"You'd better be careful, Mademoiselle Célita. When I was a boy, I had a job in the Vincennes Zoo, and at certain times of the year we weren't allowed to go in the cages of the male animals, even to clean them. Then a fortnight or three weeks later, they were as quiet as lambs, quieter than ever, as if they were trying to make up for the way they had behaved."

It didn't make her laugh. Natasha, whose partner had just left, came up to her and glanced at her watch.

"A whole hour to go! God, how my feet hurt!"

"It's not my feet," Célita answered. "It's my nerves, and I've decided to get tight."

"You think that'll help?"

"Have you heard the latest?"

"What latest? So much seems to be happening these days!"

The night before, they would willingly have jumped at each other's throat, but now they found themselves on the same side, though with different reactions. With a trace of resentment in her voice, Célita began:

"Your protégée . . ."

She stopped.

"I'm sorry."

"Go ahead. It's been a long time since I had a protégée. We have enough to do looking out for ourselves. Do you mean Maud?"

"She'll be hitting the headlines tomorrow."

"So I've heard."

"That's not all. She's going to come down here only for her number."

Incredulous, Natasha turned to Ludo, who nodded in confirmation.

"That beats everything!"

"You feel the same?"

"It won't affect me much. If they decide to sack me, I've always got a job to go to in Geneva. As for you, you'd better stop drinking, or you'll make a fool of yourself in a minute."

She hadn't needed to watch her long to see that. It was true. Célita's nerves were so taut that she needed something to make her relax, a scene, a fight, anything violent to serve as an outlet for her pent-up fury, which was choking her.

"Why don't you report sick too and go home to bed? Take a couple of sleeping pills . . ."

Ludo's advice again!

Célita was sorry the count wasn't there; she could easily have picked a quarrel with him. He irritated her enough to be a good pressure valve.

After distributing a few hats, Léon went and smoked a cigarette on the sidewalk with Emile, a thing he often did toward the end of the evening.

Célita was still bent on making some kind of scene, and she went so far as to look around for a suitable victim among the customers, but there were only two couples left in the room, and they were engrossed in each other.

She felt like going out into the street, without her coat, walking past the proprietor to the Hôtel de la Poste, and knocking on Maud's door.

"Open up, you little bitch!"

She would be forced to get out of bed and open the door, or Célita would make a terrible noise in the hallway.

"Now go back inside. Shut the door. Let's get it over with . . ."

Would Maud dare to put on her "poor little thing" act and flutter her eyelashes over her falsely innocent eyes?

Célita wanted to use her hands, her nails on the soft, too-white skin. She needed to hurt, to make her cry out, beg forgiveness.

"Now have you got it into your head that he's not for you? Answer me, girl! Answer me, you pathetic whore! Answer me, I tell you!"

She put her hand to her brow, looked across at Ludo, who shook his head, thinking she wanted another drink.

"Do you know her address in Bergerac?"

"I only know that her mother's a postmistress there."

"Is her name really Leroy?"

She was forgetting the scene she had witnessed through the peephole, when the new girl had held out her identity card to Léon and he had read her surname half aloud. If she couldn't go and fight it out with her in the Hôtel de la Poste, there was another way to get even.

When she left with Marie-Lou, half an hour later, Marie-Lou exclaimed:

"Where are we going?"

"To the post office."

One of the counters was open all night. On a form she wrote out, with a scratchy pen:

"Madame Leroy, Post Office, Bergerac, Dordogne."

Then, after pondering a moment, beneath the address wrote:

"Your daughter Maud performing in striptease show at Monico in Cannes."

"Signature?" the clerk asked, after reading it without any reaction.

She added the first name that came into her head: "Caroline Dubois," and there were no further questions.

Marie-Lou had been waiting discreetly at the door.

"You're sure you've not gone and done something silly?"

She laughed:

"It doesn't matter a hoot what I do at this stage! . . . You don't feel like getting tight?"

"No. If you're going drinking, I'm going home."

It was not really drink Célita wanted. She just wanted something to happen; it was more like some vague, unsatisfied need.

She undressed without talking. The bedroom seemed gloomier than ever, more impersonal, plainly utilitarian in a way that wasn't even aggressively ugly.

Contrary to habit, she went to bed naked, without cleaning her teeth, and it was Marie-Lou who got into bed last and turned off the light.

"Good night."

"Good night."

Minutes went past, and Célita became aware of what it was for which she had this almost painful longing: a man, any kind of man, as long as he would knock her down, hurt her, and shatter her nerves.

Perhaps it was because she had drunk too much and a kind of dislodgement was taking place in her mind, numbed between sleeping and waking. But she suddenly felt she had to get up, put on her coat, nothing else, and go and ask the first man she met in the street to relieve her need.

The night before, when she hadn't wanted it, Emile had been there.

Through the half-open window and the closed shutters, she could hear footsteps, bicycles passing, men going home from night work or starting out for their day jobs.

Her eyes open in the darkness, her body taut, her nipples hurting, she clenched her teeth, grinding them, and a long time afterward Marie-Lou's sleepy voice asked from the next bed:

"What's wrong?"

In answer, she shouted:

"Nothing! Do you hear? There's nothing wrong with me! I'm . . ."

And suddenly relaxed, empty, she burst into loud sobs.

Part Two

Chapter Six

Each of her own accord, the three of them had chosen from their wardrobes their simplest, least conspicuous dress, and they had put on hardly any makeup. There in the garden, conscious of being observed, they seemed to be imitating the gestures and demeanor of girls after High Mass.

Natasha, having arrived first, had waited for the others on the steep, narrow street where Monsieur Léon's old Pontiac was parked behind a long, low-slung sports car, bright red, which belonged to the surgeon.

When her friends looked questioningly at her, Natasha had said:

"It began a quarter of an hour ago. Apparently we can wait in the garden. And anyhow, unless something goes wrong, we won't find out much this morning."

They were at the Estérel Clinic, in a quiet old part of town, where only cats and dogs were wandering along streets sectioned into blocks of shade and sunlight, and people in a wineshop opposite were washing out bottles.

The garden, with pale gravel paths, was shaded by trees, the foliage of each a different green, and near the wall at the back some hens were clucking behind a fence.

It was unusual for them to be out of doors at such an early

hour, all together too, for it was little more than halfway through the morning, and they had had hardly any sleep. Most of the windows in the clinic were wide open, and the patients, men and women wearing cotton bathrobes with thin blue stripes, came and stared at them one after the other.

Of the three, Célita was the palest and the most anguished. During the ten days Madame Florence had spent under observation, undergoing repeated examinations, X-rays, analyses, she had come almost every afternoon at the visiting hour, and the place was now familiar to her.

She knew that the ground floor was reserved for maternity cases, and she had been in the corridor two days ago when a woman from Ward Six was being brought back, accompanied by a nurse with a bloodstained apron who was carrying a baby.

The curtain at the window occasionally swelled out with the breeze, and when it blew to one side, it revealed the bed, the mother, motionless and relaxed, some white carnations on the bedside table, and, farther inside, the child's enameled crib.

Directly above Ward Six, the windowpanes were of frosted glass, and behind those windows they were operating on the proprietress.

Natasha was also feeling a little queasy.

"Apparently, at the last moment, when they came to take her away on a stretcher, she sat up in bed screaming that she wouldn't go through with it, she'd changed her mind, she'd sooner die in peace, and she struggled so hard they had to give her two injections."

The sky was blue, the air warm and still; birds were chirping in the trees, and a blackbird, completely unafraid, was hopping about the lawn, spying with a mischievous eye on the three women.

"Where is he?" Célita asked.

"I think there's a waiting room for relatives upstairs, next to the operating theater. I didn't see him. His car was already here when I arrived."

They heard footsteps on the gravel and saw Francine, who, wearing her blue suit and with a white hat on her blond hair, walked up quickly.

"It's Thursday," she explained, "so no school, and I couldn't find anybody to look after Pierrot. I couldn't bring him here."

"What did you do?"

"He's playing in the street. There aren't many cars, and the woman in the dairy said she'd keep an eye on him through the shop window."

She, in turn, looked up at the windows with frosted panes. "Well?"

She realized nobody had any news, that they would just have to wait. After a while she asked Natasha:

"Have you heard from Ketty?"

"No. But someone saw her in Nice. That's the third person who's told me that, so it must be true. . . ."

Ketty, to everybody's surprise, had been Maud's first victim. It happened before Madame Florence entered the clinic, while she still sat behind the cash register at the Monico, for part of the night at least. Hadn't the proprietress, even then, given up hope? She was obviously seriously ill, and it had been all the more upsetting that it had happened so suddenly and had coincided with the business of Maud.

Célita, for one, was aware that the suddenness had only been apparent; Madame Florence had admitted as much to her, from her hospital bed.

"I've been expecting something to happen for a long time,"

she had confided in a gloomy voice. "That's why I used to refuse to see the doctor. I've almost always had something the matter with me inside, and I haven't been able to bear having relations with Léon for months, it hurts me so much."

In less than two weeks she had become not only a sick woman, but also exhausted, old, pitiable, her skin loose, her eyes, too large and feverish, staring as if they sought the answer to some terrifying question.

"They won't tell me what's wrong with me, but, with all the tests they've been making, I know it's cancer and I'll never get out of this bed again. . . . Poor Léon!"

She was sorry for him. She bore him no ill will, only regretted that she wouldn't be there to protect him.

"That girl *would* have to turn up at a time like this! . . . He doesn't know what to do now. He's ashamed. He hardly dares look me in the eye any longer. And he still hasn't the guts to get rid of her. . . ."

There were long silences, during which she stared at the ceiling.

"Deep down, he's a weakling. . . ."

A little later she added:

"Like all men! . . . If something does happen to me, he'll be desperately unhappy, because he'll be haunted all his life by the fear that it was his fault. . . ."

As far as the future was concerned, this was probably the truth, but for the present Célita was convinced that Léon would not be too upset if his wife disappeared from the scene. He would never admit it to himself. He would be bound to repel such a thought if it ever entered his head. It would, nonetheless, sort things out for him.

He was struggling with his life's many complications, and,

contrary to what might be supposed, all his worries were bringing him closer to Maud, instead of drawing them apart. Who knows? Perhaps he was thinking of her at this very moment, as he waited upstairs for the result of the operation.

Maud had not come, of course. He had left while she was still asleep. He spent his nights with her now, at the Louxor, formerly a luxury hotel on the Croisette, converted into furnished apartments a few years ago.

In the afternoons, the girl could be seen sunbathing on her balcony, sipping fruit juice and playing her phonograph.

She had three rooms, bright and cheerful, with a view of the sea and the beach, and she only came down, wrapped in a gown, when it was time for a swim.

Was Ketty responsible for what happened the evening after the article in *Nice-Matin* appeared, when the club was bursting with people? She had been sitting at a table in the front row with a middle-aged man who looked, and acted, like a cattle dealer or a large-scale farmer. He'd already drunk quite a lot. Wasn't it Ketty's job to make the customers drink?

It was time for the second show. Between the two shows, Maud had stayed upstairs, reading in a wicker chair installed in the dressing room for her.

It was one of those evenings that, for no apparent reason, have a more electric atmosphere than usual. Glasses had been broken at the bar, and loud remarks had greeted the flashes that went with Ketty's number.

Ketty had come downstairs after her number and gone back to the same table. Her companion's large hand, with prominent veins, was soon digging into her thigh.

That evening, Maud was evidently finding it hard to go into her trance, as they were calling it now that the reporter had used the word in his article, and this was precisely the trouble with her number: It was liable to fall flat if people didn't sense her quivering all over.

She had knelt down, the upper part of her body naked. Leaning backward, clasping her breasts, she began swaying with the music, her face agonized, her mouth twisted with the effort.

Most of the spectators, taken in, were holding their breath, but that evening there were some on whom the charm failed to work. Maud felt it, as did Gianini, who was making signs at his musicians.

In a minute, half a minute, Maud's act probably would have been successfully completed. But Ketty's companion, standing up for a better look, just as he would have done at a local fair, had called out in a croaking voice:

"Want any help, sweetheart?"

Immediately, the spell was broken, and the whole room, torn from the magic, had burst out laughing, while Maud, thrown completely off balance, tried to get up and, instead, fell awkwardly over on her side.

Léon, red with fury, had rushed forward. He had stayed a long time in the dressing room, where Maud could be heard crying, talking to her in a low voice, almost pleading with her. When he had come down again, he looked bad-tempered, and, against all the traditions of the place, he had called out in a loud voice:

"Ketty!"

Except for the cattle dealer, who sat in his place waiting for her to return, everybody had understood. When Ketty came downstairs again, she was wearing her coat and carrying her clothes over her arm, her shoes in her hand. Madame Florence, to whom her husband had hurriedly whispered something, handed her an envelope already prepared.

"Bye, girls!" she allowed herself the luxury of calling out as she left.

That night, she had slept in the rooms she shared with Natasha; the next morning, she was gone, supposedly to Geneva, where she claimed they were eagerly expecting her.

From what had been heard since, she had not even attempted to go there. She had been seen several times on the streets of Nice, around Place de la Victoire.

How had Léon managed to remain so calm and collected during all this and still to find time to devote to his new girlfriend? Everything happened at once. The very next day Madame Florence entered the clinic, and an hour later Léon received a letter asking him to present himself at the police station.

Once again Célita's idea had been a bad one. Her telegram had no more produced the desired effect than had her telephone call to the police. When Léon went to see him, the superintendent had a long letter in front of him from Maud's mother, insisting on her daughter's return.

What had gone on behind the scenes they had been able to glean only in fragments. The fact remained that only once, on the evening after Léon's visit to the police station, did Maud not appear in the cabaret. The next morning, somebody had seen the proprietor entering a lawyer's office.

Ludo, who knew about this sort of thing, had stated:

"If she's really over eighteen, they can't touch her or the boss."

Two days later, Madame Leroy had arrived in Cannes, and at three o'clock that same afternoon, because she didn't know her daughter's address, she appeared at the Monico, just when the charwomen were raising clouds of dust. Emile had spoken to her, and described her to Célita:

"A rather fat little body, dressed in black, as if she was in mourning, and a mustache."

She had spent quite a while staring at the photograph of Maud in the display box out front and was boiling with anger.

"So it's true! She's doing that! My daughter, whom I brought up as a . . . as a . . ."

She was so funny that it was hard to feel sorry for her, especially when she asked Emile:

"How much does she get paid for doing that?"

Emile had telephoned the proprietor's home to warn him. Getting no answer, he called the clinic, and finally the Hôtel de la Poste, where Maud was still living.

"Monsieur Léon? There's a lady here who insists on seeing you. . . ."

"Let me speak. I'll teach him!" little Madame Leroy burst in, trying to grab the receiver from Emile.

"No, madame . . . He's coming. . . . It's her mother, sir. . . . I keep telling her you'll be coming, but . . ."

Léon was worried that Emile might have given her Maud's address, and within a few minutes he came running up, his tie crooked, though not before he had taken the trouble to call his lawyer, who'd arrived soon afterward. Since it was impossible to talk in peace in the club with the two old women still busy working, the three of them had gone off to the lawyer's, on Mérimée Square, opposite the Casino.

Nobody knew what happened there, except that after about an hour Maud had been summoned by telephone and had joined them. What kind of scene had been played there? What bargain had they concluded? Whatever it was, Madame Leroy was never seen again at the Monico and she took the train back home the same evening.

If the proprietor had any idea who sent the telegram, he gave no sign of it. After all, even without it, Madame Leroy would have heard about her daughter sooner or later, since a Paris weekly published in its next issue, not one, but five photographs of Maud, including her "ecstasy" one, as the weekly called it, together with a gossip story about the "girl who has found her vocation as a striptease dancer."

Ketty's departure left a gap. But Madame Florence's absence from the cash register caused genuine distress, and they found themselves, to their surprise, talking in whispers and walking around on tiptoe.

The final blow, which seemed to destroy all hope of returning to normal, was Maud's move to the Louxor and the kind of ceremonial that, from then on, accompanied her arrival and departure. She never turned up now before the stroke of midnight, a few minutes before she was due to go on. The proprietor left the Monico in his car just in time to go and get her. From a branch of a famous Paris shop, he had bought her a white coat, which, as befitted her new status, she would take off at the door and hand to Francine.

What irritated Célita most was the shy, almost humble manner Maud adopted in the club, both toward the customers and with the other girls and the staff. To everyone she addressed a formal little "Good evening," as if to apologize for being there at all. Then she sat down at her table to wait for her turn, since she didn't have to change. She never failed to applaud Célita's dance, which preceded her number.

"And now, ladies and gentlemen, the management of the Monico has the pleasure and the honor . . ."

She did not always remain in the dressing room between the two shows. Sometimes she went off to the Casino, alone or with the proprietor.

Monsieur Léon, aware that, even looking on the bright side, his wife would be incapacitated for many weeks, if not months, had sent for a sister of his, whom nobody had ever heard of before, a pretty enough woman, a little too fat, a little past her best, but still appetizing, and not unlike him in looks.

She and her husband ran a café in Le Havre, near the docks, and it was noticeable in the way she sat at the cash register. But from her raucous voice, with its common undertones, and other insignificant details, which didn't escape women like the ones at the Monico, they had guessed that once upon a time she had earned her living by other means.

Unlike Madame Florence, she was never heard to say:

"Now, ladies . . ."

She called out, with false friendliness:

"Come along, girls . . ."

She was on familiar terms with them from the start.

"You, Ginger, it's time you got a move on."

"Ginger" meant Célita; Natasha had become "Lanky" and Marie-Lou "Fatty."

She had one child, a little boy about the same age as Pierrot, and she got on well with Francine. Whenever they had a moment to spare, they would be talking about measles and medicines.

Célita had not left, had not created a scene, as Natasha, in particular, had expected and as Ludo feared. She fretted a good deal, certainly, but she was careful to attack neither Léon nor the new favorite, though this didn't mean that she had given in.

Between her and Madame Florence a kind of trust had been established, even a sort of intimacy. Yet during her almost daily visits to the clinic, the two women hardly spoke, probably because they had no need of long phrases to understand each other.

Léon, moreover, was not hiding much from his wife. He told her more than Célita imagined, and for that reason Madame Florence was the first to bring up the subject of the Louxor apartment.

"I think he was right. He couldn't leave her at the Hôtel de la Poste. Do you realize how unhappy he is?"

Was she deluding herself? Was her illness depriving her of intuition, a woman's instinct, to that extent?

"You don't believe me, but it's the truth. At a certain age men are completely defenseless, even the ones who think they're so well protected; in fact, especially those. It can happen to women too. . . ."

She interrupted herself to scold Célita gently.

"Why did you bring flowers again? He sends me so many the nurse doesn't know where to put them now. It's salving his conscience, you see. I know he loves me. But it's too strong for him. . . ."

After quite a long silence she added:

"You too, you very nearly succeeded. . . . And with you I'd have been more frightened. . . ."

Hearing the proprietress talk like that, in the muted monotonous voice of a nun, Célita felt discouraged. She was left to carry on the fight alone.

Another day Madame Florence said:

"He can tell you're all against him, and that hurts him, particularly in your case. . . ."

"He said that? He mentioned me?"

Madame Florence gave no details, and Célita suspected her of lying. She could even guess the motive that prompted the proprietress to say that to her.

Even in good health, the idea might have occurred to her that they establish a common front against the enemy, leaving them free to resume the battle against each other, mercilessly, later.

Wasn't that what Célita had imagined she could read in Madame Florence's eyes the day of Maud's arrival?

Now that she was out of the game, temporarily or permanently, she didn't want Célita to give up.

If anyone was to take Léon from her, while she was alive or after her death, it must, at all costs, not be Maud.

"It's tragic, you see, for a man like him to be in a position like this, and so he's miserable. Yesterday he sat there, where you are now, and started crying, holding my hand and asking me to forgive him. . . ."

Célita pressed her nails into the palms of her hands to stop herself from crying out in anger.

Now, as she waited in the garden with her companions, thinking of the body cut open, up there on the operating table, she heard again Madame Florence's last words the day before, just as the bell was ringing for the end of the visiting hour.

"Off you go! I may never see you again. Don't be too hard on him. One day, you'll see. . . ."

It was only to her that Madame Florence had spoken like this; didn't it constitute a sort of will? With Marie-Lou, Natasha, or Francine she merely asked questions that showed she still took an interest in the cabaret, asking how many customers there had been, when they had closed; and presumably Léon's sister, Alice, gave her the figure of each day's take.

Natasha had had a talk with the chief nurse, who lived in the same building as she did. She had insisted on knowing the results of the tests, especially whether it was cancer of the uterus. Without giving a direct answer, the nurse had made a vague gesture and uttered a sigh.

"What a long time!" Marie-Lou was getting impatient. "Do you think that's a good sign?"

"Some operations last two or three hours, and even longer," Natasha replied; she knew a little about everything. "It depends on what they find."

A wizened little old man, his skull brown from the sun, was leaning on a windowsill on the third floor, wearing a patient's blue-striped bathrobe. He had waved at them two or three times.

"Do you know who he is?" asked Célita.

"I feel I've met him somewhere," Marie-Lou answered. "I don't dare look up to see for sure. Let's walk along to the end of the path, and I can have a good look on my way back. . . ."

Then she gave a little wave toward the third-floor window.

"Who is it?"

"You've never seen him; it was before your time. He owns a wholesale grocery business on Rue d'Antibes and has two sons; both are married and have children. He loves me. I used to call him grandfather, and he lapped it up.

"Only a year ago, he was still coming to the club twice a week; he had his fixed days for it. He drank only mineral water, because he was on a diet, but he always bought us a bottle of champagne, Lulu and me.

"You never knew Lulu either. She went and got married in Morocco, to somebody she met through an advertisement.

"One evening, the poor old thing saw one of his sons come in, and he rushed off to the cloakroom, where he stayed hiding for nearly two hours. He always left at midnight, whether the show was over or not, because that was the time the café shut where he was supposed to be playing cards."

In this way they tried to keep their minds off what was happening behind the frosted-glass windows. Each time they passed, they paused a moment outside Ward Six, where the young mother was now giving her baby the breast.

"If Madame Florence died . . ." Marie-Lou began.

"Touch wood!" Francine exclaimed.

And Célita also touched the little twig the other woman picked up.

"You're right. Let's not think about it . . ."

But immediately they started thinking about it, not only out of pity for Madame Florence, but because their livelihood was at stake. Once Léon was free to do what he pleased, would he keep the Monico? And even if he did, wasn't it likely, the way he was behaving now, that he would soon be forced to shut down?

Célita suspected Ludo of following the course of events with special interest and of having his eye on the nightclub. It might be his opportunity to step into the boss's shoes. He was divorced; his son was grown up and doing his military service. If Célita, in whom he showed a marked interest, were to maneuver skillfully . . .

She rejected the thought as soon as it entered her head, not only because now wasn't the time for it, when Madame Florence was lying there with her stomach cut open, but also because she knew it would never work.

It was not so much security she was looking for. Security was only of secondary importance. The most important thing was that she no longer had any wish to live without a man, that she had decided this man was Léon, and that she refused to give up.

There was one person who had seen through her better than her friends, better even than Madame Florence, and, strangely, this person had never had a real conversation with her and hardly knew her.

This was the Comte de Despierres, who had been in a lot during the last few days, invariably sitting at the bar and watching people coming and going with his irritating smile. Célita thought he came to see her, since she was always the one he bought drinks for. He asked few questions, and when he did, they were brief, cynical. Was it Ludo, with whom she sometimes saw him gossiping across the bar, who kept him informed?

Once, for example, he had simply asked:

"Not dead yet?"

"Are you speaking of the proprietress?" she had replied severely.

"That'll be one of them out of your way, won't it?"

She hated him, and yet she could not help going over to join him as soon as he beckoned.

"How are the lovers getting on? No jewels yet?"

"She's too smart for that."

"But, you see, her heart's not set on having that place at the cash register."

"How do you know?"

"I can see through her as well as I can see through you. That's all I need."

"Because you're so intelligent, I suppose? So very superior and intelligent . . ."

"I'm not sure about that, but I know women. As far as that girl's concerned, she's just using the proprietor of the Monico as a stepping stone. He can help her over the first step, which is the most difficult. She knows very well she's got to smooth away her rough edges, and before she aims higher she'll need a halo."

The idea of a halo made her laugh.

"Let's say, if you like, a past that is more or less spicy, a good wardrobe, some jewels, entrée to the Casino, and probably a car . . ."

Célita gazed at him with wide, staring eyes, struck by the truth of his remarks, and he went on in a careless tone, like a conjurer condescending to do a few card tricks:

"At thirty-two"—and he pointed his cigarette toward the cash register—"you might want that seat over there. Not at nineteen. At nineteen that would be considered sheer burial alive. Then, you imagine you're going much further."

He stubbed out his cigarette in a club ashtray.

"And she will go further!"

She wondered whether Léon, who was watching them from across the room and frowning, guessed that he was the indirect subject of the conversation. Rather than let the count see that he had impressed her, she preferred to murmur nonchalantly:

"I didn't know you went in for fortune-telling."

She only really understood two days later, when she had to undergo, in her heart of hearts, a humiliating experience.

Curiously, the state of nervous excitement in which she had been living since Maud's arrival had been accompanied by a parallel sexual excitement, and one afternoon when Marie-Lou was on the beach, she had not sent Emile away when he hoisted himself up onto the windowsill from the street.

Emile now had more free time, because the boss did not come so regularly to the Monico during the afternoons. He was sometimes even seen in a pair of bathing trunks, lying stretched out next to Maud on the Louxor beach.

Célita suspected that Emile, to save time, got rid of many of his fliers by throwing them down drains.

He always came with a piece of news for her. He was the only one who ever went to the Louxor apartment, on errands, and he had found Léon, in his pajamas, reading the paper in a chair on the balcony.

"He didn't seem to mind my seeing him like that. He even showed me the bedroom and said:

" 'Cozy, isn't it?' "

Emile was no longer so deeply moved when Célita complied with his wishes, but he showed his satisfaction with exuberance.

"Gee, you're a nice girl! And your skin's so soft!"

Célita, more and more often, aspired to something better. Why didn't the count, who intrigued and repelled her at the same time, make some move? The idea of making love with him, even though she despised him, did not displease her.

She had many times considered it, telling herself that, since he came back so often and never took any notice of the others, he must have considered it too.

One evening, to test the water, she murmured, as she lightly pressed her breast against the man's arm, almost inadvertently:

"You're always talking about women, and you know such a lot about them. Yet you don't seem to do much about it. . . ."

At once, from the smile that lit up the man's face, from a sense of relief she detected in him, she had a glimmer of the truth.

"That's just it!" he said, wrinkling his eyelids. "I have an infinite appreciation for women, and they can be exquisite friends. All my life I've regretted not having a sister. Why, nothing would give me greater pleasure than your coming one afternoon and having a cup of tea with me on the Croisette."

And then, since she was still not sure what he was implying:

"When did you guess that I am an invert?"

He didn't say "homosexual," but used a term that was more elegant somehow, and scientific at the same time.

"You look disappointed."

"Why should I be disappointed?"

"I could be an excellent friend for you, because you're as complicated a creature as one could wish for, and what fascinates me most about you is that you have all the vices. I once had a friend who . . ."

"Thank you."

"It was meant as a compliment."

He realized something had gone wrong, that the spell, if there had been a spell, was broken.

"I'm very sorry. I was mistaken."

His last words were:

"It's a great pity."

He did not return to the Monico, and Célita preferred not to think about him any more.

"Couldn't we go and ask if it's over yet?" Marie-Lou asked. She was anxious to get back to bed.

It was eleven o'clock. Madame Florence had been on the operating table for nearly two hours. Maud was probably still asleep, or at least in her reclining chair on the balcony, watching the multicolored specks of bathers on the sand and the sails gliding across the bay.

What none of them could guess was that, at that moment, Léon had gone out into the corridor on the second floor and stopped a nurse as she went by.

"Do you know where I can find a telephone?"

"Try the office on the ground floor."

There he timidly asked permission to use the telephone, gave the Louxor number, which he knew by heart, and was obliged to speak in the presence of the secretary.

"Is that you? . . . Yes . . . No, it's not over yet. . . . No! Nobody can tell me a thing. . . . The door's shut. . . ."

His voice became softer, almost a whisper, as he added:

"I won't be long."

It was said so tenderly that he might just as well have said "darling."

"Are you waiting for Number Seventeen?"

"Yes."

"Didn't anyone tell you it'll be another hour? If there's anything you have to do . . ."

He was tempted, but resisted. As he walked past the front door, at the foot of the stairs, he noticed the four women waiting in the garden, and, sulkily, he muttered some unkind words to them, as if he felt the only reason for their coming was to make him feel guilty.

He didn't dare smoke inside, so he had been intending to have a cigarette on the entrance steps; now he preferred to go without.

It did not take quite an hour, only forty minutes, but the four women were so tired of standing, their feet were so sore, that they had finally sat down on a bench, as if they were in a public garden.

It had never entered their heads that there was another entrance to the clinic. Suddenly, Natasha heard the surgeon's red car start, and Léon's almost immediately afterward.

"Why don't you go in?"

They sent Célita off to reconnoiter. She made her way to the office, forcing herself not to look into the wards, whose doors were all open.

"Are you for Number Seventeen?"

"Yes, madame."

"She can't be seen today, and it's not certain yet whether the doctor will allow any visitors tomorrow. I should warn you that it's highly unlikely."

"The operation?"

The woman in the office, whose job it was to record, in a number of columns, all the births, illnesses, and deaths, looked at Célita as if she had asked something ridiculous.

"It's over, naturally."

"But . . ."

"She's still under the effects of the anesthetic and she'll sleep till this evening."

"Is the doctor at all hopeful?"

This word did not seem to have the same meaning for the secretary as it does for ordinary mortals; perhaps it meant absolutely nothing to her, since she simply looked at Célita, her eyes without expression.

"I suppose we ought not to send any flowers?"

"Until further notice, certainly not."

"Couldn't I just see her, even through a crack in the door?"

"Impossible."

"Thank you."

She rejoined the others in the garden, and the four of them moved off toward the iron gates, where Marie-Lou remembered to wave her hand at the little old man on the third floor.

"Well?"

"Nothing, except that she's alive. They say she'll sleep till this evening."

"And then?"

Célita merely shrugged her shoulders, and Marie-Lou declared:

"As far as I'm concerned, I need a drink before I go and do the same. I'll treat you all."

In a nearby street they found a little bar, where people came in the evening to play bowls but which was empty at this time of day. The owner, in his shirtsleeves, had been reading the paper in an easy chair, which was occupied by the cat when he was interrupted. He looked in some bewilderment at these rare women customers, who all chose vermouth because he didn't have their regular drinks.

Marie-Lou had the last word:

"She'll pull through all right, trust me. And before a month's over you'll see her doling out the fines to me because the polish on my toenails is chipped or I've been eating garlic. Let's have the same again, Arthur!"

Chapter Seven

For a long time now, ever since Maud's arrival at the Monico, Célita had been trying to make some sort of contact with Léon, but, whether deliberately or not, he was continually slipping away from her. When she arrived in the evening, if he was already there, he nodded to her in the same way as he did to the others, seeming preoccupied, and if, during the course of the night, he had anything to say to her concerning her work, it was brief and to the point.

Once afternoon, before Madame Florence had her operation, he had arrived at the clinic while Célita was sitting at her bedside. After kissing his wife on the forehead, he had gone over to stand in front of the window; he did not move from there for the rest of her visit.

Day after day, she would watch carefully for a chance to get him to herself at last. She had nothing particular to say to him, she was not hoping for anything from him, but she could not bear to live with this hostile vacuum between them.

A dozen times she had been on the point of making a scene at the height of the evening's entertainment, and this might have been a relief. She purposely infringed all the sacrosanct rules, under his very eyes, as if to defy him: going out during the show to have a breath of fresh air on sidewalk; or, when she knew she was being watched, refusing to dance with a good customer on the excuse that her feet were hurting.

She never managed to be alone with him, and it would scarcely have helped to go to the Monico in the afternoon. She would have to be very lucky to choose one of the rare days on which he now went there then, and, in any case, the charwomen would be there, or delivery men.

Natasha left, and her absence changed the atmosphere once again. Probably everybody, Léon included, had the feeling that it was the beginning of the end.

Performers had come and gone, of course, replacing each other in more or less rapid succession during the last few years, but that had been due to the normal need for a different program; this time, it was more like rats leaving a sinking ship.

For Natasha, the whole thing had happened within two evenings, in the most unexpected way. They had all noticed a young man at the bar, very dark, Asiatic-looking, who knew only a few words of French, but, according to Natasha, spoke very good English without a trace of an accent.

She kept him company until closing time, and after having a snack at Justin's, she let herself be taken out for a run in a motorboat with him, just as day was breaking.

The next evening, he was there when they opened, correct and shy, and Natasha showed the others his picture, which had recently appeared in *Nice-Matin*. He was an Iranian prince, a genuine one, a cousin of the shah, who had studied at Cambridge and was now spending a few weeks in France. He had been photographed with the prefect, who had welcomed him when he arrived by plane.

As she was getting dressed for the first show, Natasha announced:

"Guess what he wants me to do? First he asked if I knew Paris well, the Louvre and the museums and all; then he offered me a hundred thousand francs, and all expenses, if I would be his guide and interpreter for a month. What would you do, if you were me?"

The Iranian waited for her answer until the second show, smiling, courteous, getting up to offer Natasha a stool each time she went over to join him.

Eventually she informed the others:

"I've said yes, dears. If things were different here, I might have hesitated, but the way the club's going now . . ."

"When are you leaving?"

"Tomorrow, by car. He's bought an Italian racing car and he's already reserved an apartment at the Plaza. . . ."

"Have you told the boss the news?"

"Not yet. I'll tell him when I go."

Would Célita have tried to seize an opportunity like that if she had known English? Probably. All at once, Natasha was escaping from their world, and they caught themselves looking at her with something like respect.

Immediately after her departure, Léon called Francine as she was getting ready to go home.

"From tomorrow, you'll have to do your number again, for a few days."

Célita and Marie-Lou were already on their way to Place du Commandant-Maria. They were almost ready for bed when they heard somebody tapping on the shutters. It was poor Francine, very upset, wanting to tell them her news.

She had twice tried to do a striptease number, several months before, and Madame Florence had told her, bluntly:

"You'd better stick to the cloakroom, Francine. You make yourself look like a dirty picture."

It was true. When fully dressed, Francine made the best impression; without any effort, she could pass for a pleasant, attractive little housewife. Once naked, she looked like one of those buxom nudes you see in paintings in art galleries, her pink flesh forming plump curves, by no means uncomely.

Unfortunately, there was the business of transformation— in other words, the act of taking her clothes off—and although she did her best to follow the rhythm of the music, everything would go wrong. She became absurd, not to say indecent, and the G-string, whether it was of pink or black satin, appeared erotic and shocking beneath her rounded belly.

"I couldn't say I wouldn't do it. He seemed so upset. He said that everyone was letting him down and that I was the only one he could depend on. . . ."

And to Célita:

"Do you mind if I come over tomorrow, so you can tell me what to do?"

So they rehearsed a number there, between the uncleared table and the Henri II sideboard. To replace Francine in the cloakroom while he waited for a Paris agency to send him a new performer, Léon hired an old woman with a thin, lugubrious face, who normally sold national lottery tickets in cafés.

The musicians had taken advantage of the situation to ask for a raise, to which the proprietor had finally agreed, after a violent angry outburst.

And Célita continued to wait for her turn, watching for a favorable moment to accost him.

On Sunday, when he returned from driving Maud back to the Louxor in his car, he stepped onto the sidewalk and found himself face to face with Célita, who had ostensibly come out to smoke a cigarette.

"What do you think you're doing here, eh?"

Emile discreetly moved a few paces away from them.

"I was waiting for you, Monsieur Léon."

She called him Monsieur Léon as if they were still in the club, not standing outside in the street. Did he think she wanted to make trouble? At all events, he started to go straight in the door, and when she barred his way, there was a resigned look on his face.

"I suppose you want a raise too?" he muttered a little bitterly.

"No. I simply want your permission to go and see Madame Florence."

Madame Florence had spent another week in the clinic after the operation and had been taken home by ambulance three days earlier. Since then, Célita had not dared go to see her, because she would have been no longer on neutral ground, but in Madame Florence's own home. Emile was the only one ever to have been inside the flat on Boulevard Carnot.

Léon looked her sternly in the eyes. He hesitated, realizing perhaps that it would be better to keep quiet, but his rancor got the better of him, probably because his own conscience was not clear, and he said:

"If you're counting on taking her place, you're wasting your time."

Without waiting to think, without knowing what she was doing, her features hardened and she slapped him, standing stiff on her high heels. He seized her wrist and twisted it, as she spat in his face:

"Aren't you ashamed of yourself? Tell me!"

It was as if she had recovered her real personality, her real temperament.

"And you, you little bitch, weren't you ashamed of yourself when you were doing your level best to try to take her place?"

Aware that they were separated from the customers by only a velvet curtain, and still holding her wrist in a way that hurt, he spoke in a low voice, close to her, so close that their breath mixed, a look of hatred on his face:

"Do you want me to remind you of all the things you've done, all the things you've said?"

At that moment she still regarded him as an equal, but he uttered a sentence, just one, that forced Célita to close her eyes and give up the struggle:

"Do you want me to remind you about the sleeping pills? Do you, you whore?"

He saw that she had given up and brusquely let go of her, giving her a push that almost threw her against the wall.

"Go and see Florence as often as you like, but get any idea out of your head that you'll ever take her place at the cash register!"

She didn't burst into tears. Avoiding Emile, who longed for a sign that he could comfort her, she started walking alone toward the end of the street, beside the line of parked cars.

The sleeping-pill business had been a mistake, and she had realized as much almost at once, but she had never imagined Léon would dare throw it in her face, because there were even more unpleasant truths she could fling back at him.

It was a dirty trick to play, and he wouldn't be feeling proud of the way he had just extricated himself. Didn't that prove what a mess he had made of his life since Maud had got him in her clutches?

It had happened the previous Christmas. At the Monico, the party had gone on until half past five in the morning, and everybody had had a lot to drink, including Célita, and even Léon, who usually remained sober.

Léon had done something quite out of character, since, at any rate at the club, he took his role as proprietor very seriously.

Had Célita looked more desirable than on other evenings, or was it the alcohol that made him behave as he had? At four o'clock, a time when she had no business in the dressing room, since the shows were finished, he had whispered to her:

"Go upstairs and wait till I come."

He had finally joined her, there among the costumes lying around untidily, and she had seen an expression on his face that she was more used to seeing on the faces of his customers.

"Our own little Christmas . . ." he had whispered in her ear before he took her, the whole time watching the cloakroom below through the fanlight at floor level.

Had Madame Florence guessed what had been going on when she saw them coming back one after the other? A little later, she had simply said:

"You'd better fasten your dress properly, Célita."

The next morning, Célita only vaguely remembered how she had got home. A customer had driven her off, with Marie-Lou and another man, and for a long time they had stayed in the car, which he had parked at the end of the jetty, nobody saying a word, the darkness outside blurred by fine rain.

The way the night had ended disgusted her, that and then the fact that Marie-Lou, at eleven o'clock, was already up, almost fresh-looking, putting on some cologne before going out to lunch at the Napoule with a woman friend of hers who was married and had children.

She could not get back to sleep, caught in the grip of a depression such as she had rarely known before. She had never felt so dirty, physically and morally, and though she could not remember anything about it, she knew that if she opened her handbag she would find a crumpled ten-thousand-franc note in it, which she probably had begged from her last partner.

Outside, people were returning home from Mass, families with children walking in front holding each other by the hand, and inside the houses there would be the warm smell of turkey or black pudding.

Marie-Lou, when she left, had forgotten to close the kitchen shutters, and through the connecting door, which was ajar, Célita could see from her bed a grayish rectangle of falling rain.

She tried to go back to sleep. Her head ached, her whole body ached. She was ashamed of herself, frightened of the future, seeing no reason why it should be any better than the past or the present.

She twisted and turned in the sheets, and the pillow was clammy. When she got out of bed to drink a glass of water, she noticed, on the shelf in the bathroom, the sleeping pills, which she sometimes used.

She took two, hoping they would make her sleep at last and stop thinking, but instead of putting her right out, as usual, the drug plunged her into a half-dazed state.

In vain she struggled to sink more deeply into unconsciousness. Each time, she returned, not to the surface, but to middle water, water as dull and dispiriting as the rectangle of gray rain.

Her thoughts were disconnected, however, though they did not become fantastic, as they do in dreams, and they even seemed rational. Since she loathed herself, since life wasn't offering her, and never would offer her, anything clean and pleasant, why not simply end it?

At the Monico, Léon had taken her as he might a whore, and what she had done subsequently was to act like a whore again. Was that what she was to become, at thirty-two, now that she no longer had any chance to rise, but every chance to slip still lower, right to the gutter?

If, instead of two sleeping pills, she had taken six, or eight, or . . .

She would feel no pain. She would fall asleep, and that evening Léon would realize, too late, what he had lost.

She imagined Marie-Lou's return home, her screams, the demented landlady bursting in, people calling the police and the doctor, Léon hurrying over, Madame Florence having pangs of remorse, and, later, at the club, mournful whispering.

Then there would be the funeral, with the whole staff walking behind the hearse, even the musicians.

The passersby would stop and say:

"It's that girl who used to dance at the Monico. . . ."

Later, she had preferred to suppress the memory of that afternoon.

If it hadn't been Christmas, if it hadn't been raining, if she hadn't got drunk the night before, and if there hadn't been that episode in the car at the end of the jetty, probably nothing would have happened.

Why, to crown everything, did Marie-Lou have to go out to lunch with someone from a proper family?

Célita was alone in the world, huddled in a not very clean bed, staring at the window, unable to go peacefully to sleep, when suddenly an idea came into her head that would have appeared preposterous to anybody in their right senses.

She had taken only two pills, but she might have taken more; nobody could know. When she had thought of dying, hadn't she chiefly wanted to make Léon feel sorry?

It was not as clear as that, but that was the sense of her reasoning.

If Léon should hear that she was dying, wouldn't she achieve the same result, with the difference that she would be there to profit from it?

It was simple, as long as she planned the details and the setting suitably, and she pondered over it for nearly an hour.

Eventually, with her face haggard and seeming to totter, which demanded no great effort, she went to knock on the door of the old landlady, who lived alone at the other end of the hall. When it opened, she stood propped against the wall, in a theatrical pose, and spoke with difficulty:

"Please call Monsieur Tourmaire at once and tell him I'm feeling very ill, that I'm scared I'm going to die. . . ."

At the Monico, they almost always used Christian names, but Léon did possess a surname.

"Do you know his number?"

"It's in the book. He lives at 57 Boulevard Carnot."

She swayed, and the old lady had to support her on her way back to bed.

"Is there anything I can do?"

Yet the landlady had never liked either her or Marie-Lou,

because of the underwear they hung outside the window, which had been the cause of innumerable arguments.

"Hello! Monsieur Tourmaire? . . . This is Mademoiselle Perrin's landlady. . . . What? . . ."

Célita's surname was unfamiliar to him, although he must have read it on her papers. It was better known to Madame Florence, because she had to fill it in every month on the national insurance forms.

"Mademoiselle Célita then . . . She says she's feeling very ill, that she's going to die, and she wants you to come right away."

That wasn't exactly right. The landlady was talking too much, and Célita was beginning to regret her playacting.

"He's coming. Where is it you feel ill?"

"Everywhere . . . Here especially . . ."

She pointed to her stomach, her abdomen.

"I'll get you a hot-water bottle."

Léon took scarcely a quarter of an hour to get there and was very alarmed.

"What's happened?"

Indicating the old lady, she murmured in a weak voice:

"Tell her to get out!"

Pretending to suffer a spasm, then another, she pointed at the bottle of pills, which she had placed in full view on the bedside table.

He became still more upset, but in a different way, as if he suddenly realized his responsibilities and the consequences this business might have for him.

"I'll call a doctor."

It was plain that he wasn't anxious to do so.

"No . . . not the doctor . . ." she begged.

She was clinging to the man's large hand as if he alone could prevent her dying.

"I didn't want to bring you. . . . But I didn't have the courage to go without seeing you again."

"Have you vomited?"

"No."

"You must vomit. Get out of bed."

"I can't."

He got a bowl from the kitchen and made Célita sit on the edge of the bed.

"Stick your finger down your throat . . . Right down . . . Once more . . ."

She obeyed, her face crimson, her eyes wet.

"Go on . . . You've got to be sick. . . . If you can't manage it, I'll take you to the hospital."

She vomited, bitter liquid, for the most part. He handed her a glass of water.

"Drink this and do it again. It'll wash out your stomach."

Three times he made her drink and throw up the liquid.

"I saw them do this once in a case like this, one evening in Montmartre. One of the girls had . . ."

This memory that now came back to him was to spoil everything. He looked at her more intently, felt her pulse, stared at her eyes, and lifted her eyelids as he had seen the doctor do.

She had forgotten that a man who had spent much of his life in and out of Montmartre would have seen almost everything.

"How many pills did you take?"

"I can't remember. . . ."

She was still striving to win.

"Six perhaps . . . Or it may have been only five. . . ."

"Or was it just one? Come on, admit it!"

She shook her head furiously.

"Two?"

What could she do but change her tactics and burst into sobs? Since he wasn't going to believe her tale, she had better tell him the truth and make it sound pathetic.

"Ever since this morning, when Marie-Lou woke me up as she was getting dressed, I've been thinking of you, picturing you at home with another woman, your wife, because she was the one who had the luck to meet you when you were still free, while I . . ."

He had listened to her right to the end, and she had said a great deal more, her breast heaving, carried away by her own game, not really knowing any more when she was being melodramatic and when sincere.

"Every night when I leave, I watch you going off with her. . . ."

She sensed he was weakening, then hardening himself again, only to weaken once more, and it was then that she staked everything.

"I know I'm a bitch. I hate your wife and I won't be happy till the day she's gone. You want the whole truth? Well, if I could murder her and be sure of not getting caught, I'd do it without turning a hair. I hate myself for it, but I want you and I'd do anything to get you. . . . Last night, when you had me in your arms, I almost called out to her to come and see us, to show her that you were mine as well as hers, to shout at her that I'm the one you love. . . . That's what you said, didn't you? . . . Answer me!"

Between his teeth, he snarled:

"Little slut!"

And he slapped her, then flung himself on her, viciously.

That day she had not been sure whether she had won or lost. When he was dressed again, he was visibly disturbed, and though he had often returned in the following months, he never referred to what had happened that day.

Had he at last given her the answer, just now, when he had spat at her:

"Do you want me to remind you about the sleeping pills? Do you, you whore?"

She must calm down. She would not leave. She would leave only if she was thrown out by brute force. And then it would be the sleeping pills for good and all, because then she'd have nothing more to lose.

All these cars, some of them worth thousands of francs, belonged to men, even to married couples, who had paid to see four women take their clothes off, and especially to see Maud perform her dirty little act for them, in which she thrilled herself as she threw men into excitement at the sight of her naked body.

"What I could do to that bitch!" she muttered under her breath, alone in the middle of the sidewalk.

One day—she was sure of this, she had to feel sure of it— she would have a chance to get her own back. Till then it was essential to keep calm, to preserve complete calm.

"Calm down, Célita, calm down!" she repeated to herself like an incantation.

And her features did gradually resume their normal expression. She was even able to force a smile for Emile's benefit, when he looked at her, a little frightened.

"Well, did you hear me slap his face?"

Léon did not fire her there and then, which meant that he would not do so at all. Consequently, all was not lost.

The very next morning she rang the bell of the Tourmaires' flat, in a prosperous-looking yellowish stucco house of the type built in Cannes fifty years ago. There was a marble staircase; the doors were of a dark wood, fitted with brass handles.

A young girl, not more than sixteen, with untidy hair and a dirty face, opened the door to her.

"I want to see Madame Florence, please. Tell her it's Célita."

"I'll ask the nurse. If you'll wait in here . . ."

She showed her into a room with polished furniture of no particular style. With its rugs and ornaments, lithographs and portraits on the walls, andirons and brass fender in front of the fireplace, it might have been the living room of some retired couple with ample means.

Léon and Florence, who had spent most of their lives in the chaos of Montmartre and still lived on the fringe of decent society, had obviously done their best to establish more reassuring surroundings at home. Heavy drapes framed the windows, and through the short muslin curtains the motionless foliage of plane trees in the sun could be seen.

A strong-looking woman with masculine features, wearing a short white coat, appeared in the doorway.

"You may go in and see Madame Tourmaire, but please do not stay more than ten minutes, and don't let her talk more than is absolutely necessary, because the slightest effort tires her."

"How is she?"

The nurse put a finger to her lips, pointed to the half-open door, and said in a louder voice, which the sick woman would hear:

"The convalescence is taking its usual course, and the doctor is quite satisfied with her progress so far. Now, as always after these operations, it's simply a question of time, patience, and will power."

They had started lying to the invalid, and that was a bad sign. Célita sensed this and her heart grew heavy. Yet it was true that a few months earlier she had longed for her death, and would have been capable of carrying out what she had told Léon.

With illness it was another matter, and Célita could not help thinking that one day she might be in her place.

Madame Florence's eyes, in her colorless face, were even larger and more pathetic than at the clinic, and Célita felt a sort of repulsion as she held the hot moist hand that emerged from beneath the sheet to take hers. Most of all, she noticed the smell in the room, which was not the smell of medicine, but a human smell, which came from the bed and oppressed her so much that she dared not breathe deeply.

"Monsieur Léon gave me permission to come; otherwise I would not have thought of disturbing you."

"Sit down."

The voice came from far away. The eyes indicated a cane-seated chair, and Célita noticed a crucifix above the walnut bed, which was the same style as the wardrobe with two mirrors that stood between the windows.

"I gather you mustn't talk too much and I really only came to tell you that everything's fine at the Monico. Dear old Francine is not doing too badly; some of the customers seem to like her. Yesterday I told her to do a really comic number, but she doesn't dare. We're expecting a new dancer from Paris. . . ."

She was talking for the sake of talking, because Madame Florence's fixed stare disconcerted her. Besides, the nurse was still there, in an armchair by the window.

"It's getting hot already. The season's begun, and the Croisette is swarming with tourists. Cars have to just creep along. . . ."

Why did Madame Florence look as though she were laughing at her? It was barely noticeable, the slightest curve of her pale lips.

"You'll be up and about by the height of summer, when we'll need you more than ever . . . ."

She went on, saying anything that came into her head:

"It's amazing how well Madame Alice gets along. . . ."

Perhaps that was a blunder, since Alice, who was only her sister-in-law, had taken her place at the cash register.

"Though of course it's not the same without you. All the regulars ask after you. You must get well soon. . . ."

She was losing heart. Her thoughts tumbled over each other. Perhaps she was being affected by the idea that this was the room where Léon and Florence slept together.

Suddenly she felt further from her ambition than ever; the whole atmosphere was so weird. Emile had said to her:

"They've got a marvelous flat, with carpets everywhere."

She had not imagined it like this. It was as if she had discovered a different Florence, another Léon.

At the Monico, they belonged, although on a higher level, to the same sort of group as she did, the same world. With the proprietor in the club or standing at the entrance, and Madame Florence at the cash register, the ties one felt linked them were ties that could be broken.

Here, in spite of the absence of children, they were not only a married couple, but also a family. In black-and-gold oval frames were two portraits, of an old man and an old lady in clothes of around 1900.

"Is that your mother?" she asked foolishly.

The woman, with gray hair done in a tight bun on the top of her head, was wearing a whaleboned bodice and had a cameo brooch pinned on her bosom. She had the angular and stubborn features of a peasant.

Madame Florence shook her head and murmured:

"Léon's grandmother. She brought him up; his sister too."

She looked toward the mantelpiece, and Célita walked over to it to find a rather blurred photograph of a chubby little boy, holding a hoop in his hand.

"When he was six . . ." Madame Florence whispered.

The nurse stood up, indicating that it was time to leave.

"If my visits don't upset you, I'll come and see you again. . . ."

She felt that Madame Florence wanted to say something to her, but didn't dare, perhaps through modesty, perhaps because of the presence of the nurse.

"Till then . . ."

She was accompanied out, but she was reluctant to leave; it seemed to her that something had been left undone. She didn't know what, but she felt vaguely uneasy about it.

"May I really come again?" she asked the nurse.

"You'd better telephone before you do. We're giving her injections to make her sleep as much as possible."

In a hardly audible voice, she asked again:

"Is there any hope?"

The answer was neither yes nor no. Just a vague shrug of the shoulders.

That night the new girl arrived from Paris, a blonde with regular features and a body that was more perfect, though less statuesque, than Natasha's. She appeared with a suitcase full of makeup articles and showed her surprise and disappointment when she saw the lack of amenities in the communal dressing room.

"Aren't there any closets where we can put our things?"

"You've got to hang them on the rod behind the curtain."

"What about our underclothes?"

Célita showed her the fiber boxes balanced on a plank.

"It looks pretty miserable to me."

"It *is* miserable," Célita agreed.

The new girl called herself Gilda, but her real name was Emma Willenstein. She had appeared in two or three classy cabarets in Paris, and she showed them the programs.

"Who's the star performer advertised outside? Isn't she here?"

"She only turns up when it's time for her act, and she leaves right away afterward."

Gilda must have lived in France or Belgium for a long time, since she spoke French fluently, with an accent that was hard to place at first, because, although she had been born in Cologne, her mother was a Czech.

"They told me I could rent the rooms of the girl who left. . . . But I don't reckon I'll stay around in this moldy spot more than a week or two. I've got an engagement for July and August at Ostend. . . ."

That evening everybody's eyes were on her, from the bartender to the band, in the way one always watches a newcomer. Célita didn't object when she was told her number would come before Gilda's, which meant a step downward in the hierarchy for her.

The German girl's dress, of thick white silk, with a skirt as wide as a crinoline, must have cost a lot of money, and her act was studied, a new one for Cannes, because, instead of the traditional G-string, she finished up completely naked, hiding the vital parts with a feather fan, which she mimed her readiness to close if the audience demanded it.

Maud applauded, as she had always applauded Célita, and Léon looked across as if to ask her permission to go and congratulate the new recruit in the cloakroom. He stayed there only a few seconds and was leaning against the door when Gianini finished announcing Maud Le Roy, as, accompanied by a clash of cymbals, she advanced onto the floor.

A little later, Gilda came downstairs, looked around for Célita, and went and sat at her table. It was as if she had made her choice. For, just as everybody will stare at a newcomer, wondering whether they will like her, the newcomer is always a little lost and needs help in getting acclimated to the club.

"I watched her number through the little window."

She meant what they called the peephole.

"I suppose she sleeps with the boss."

"Ssh! She's his official mistress. . . ."

"And at the register, is that his wife?"

"His sister. His wife's ill; she's just had an operation."

"Funny sort of joint! What's he done all his life?"

"He was a bartender in Montmartre for ages."

"And the fat girl, who looks as though she needs a bath?"

Two or three times during the course of the evening she repeated:

"Funny sort of joint!"

Finally Célita grew so irritated by it that she kept out of her way. In a sense, this "joint" had almost come to be her home, and up until quite lately they had really considered themselves members of a family, with a family's loves, hates, jealousies.

Célita knew better than anybody how everything had changed, but it did not make it any less disagreeable to have a stranger take it upon herself to tell her, while looking around the place in a sarcastic, disdainful way.

Anyway, it was plain that she must have come from a funny sort of jont herself, for, at about three o'clock in the morning, she left the American with the crew cut and the white linen suit with whom she had been sitting, and went across to the bar to whisper something in Ludo's ear. Ludo shook his head and sent her over to Monsieur Léon, who was standing near the door. He also said no to her.

Célita could guess what had happened without having to listen to Gilda, who, with an angry look, had just told her boyfriend.

The new girl had supposed she would be allowed to leave before closing time to accompany the American to his hotel.

The American obviously did not want to sit there drinking champagne while he waited for her, because she wrote something down for him on a piece of paper, which he slipped into his pocket before he left, giving Léon a sulky look as he went by.

Now that the summer holidays had begun, the customers were different, noisier and more vulgar; less champagne was consumed, and every night one or another complained about being charged a thousand francs for a bottle of beer they could buy for a hundred francs in a café.

"Don't forget there's a floor show," Jules would explain each time, and some of them would take their revenge by not giving him a tip.

Francine was talking of taking a month off to go with her little boy to the mountains.

The club was slowly emptying. It was half past three. Célita sat alone at a table, thinking of nothing in particular, vaguely watching Marie-Lou yawning while a white-haired man chattered to her incessantly, at the same time busily kneading her fat thigh with his hand.

At one moment the light seemed to fade, a thing that often happened when there was a storm in the mountains.

A few minutes later, the telephone rang by the cash register, and Alice lifted the receiver. At first it seemed that she could not hear because of the music; she glanced over toward the door. What she was saying could not be heard either, certainly not by Célita, who was sitting near the band. She saw Alice hesitate, then get up and pass behind Ludo, to whom she whispered a few words.

Ludo, frowning, looked from the proprietor to Célita, while Alice leaned over the end of the bar to speak to her brother, whom she had beckoned over.

Célita, holding her breath, did not move, but missed nothing that was happening. When she saw Léon rush out without a word to anybody, she felt her hands turn icy cold.

Her eyes must have been eloquent; through the crowd, the noise, the streamers hanging from the ceiling, Ludo understood her unspoken question, answered her with a movement of his eyelids as he took a bottle of brandy and poured himself a full glass.

Madame Florence was dead.

Chapter Eight

There had been a violent storm the previous night, and the air was clean and transparent, so that in the far distance every detail of the mountains was visible, the little white houses standing out in relief as in stereoscopic views. At a very early hour, some of the residents of La Californie and Le Cannet were able to see Corsica, whose peaks made a jagged line in the merging turquoise blue of sea and sky.

At quarter to ten it was already hot and hazy, and women in shorts were coming down Boulevard Carnot, toward the market, glancing curiously at the little groups of people standing under the plane trees, aware that something was going to happen. Not until they reached Number 57 did they discover the black drapes with the fringes and silver drops. Some of the women crossed themselves.

The people waiting were mainly men, proprietors of cabarets or bars from Juan-les-Pins, Nice, and also from the other side of the Estérel: Saint-Raphaël, Saint-Tropez, Toulon, and Marseille. Most of them looked lost at being up and about so early, and some of the faces seemed familiar, as if they had appeared in the papers, in odd items of local news.

Célita arrived with Marie-Lou and Francine, and they joined Ludo, Jules, and Gianini on the sidewalk.

"Have you been upstairs?"

Ludo nodded, and they in turn went into the house, as each of the others had done before going out to wait in the street. They climbed the staircase, stopping on the landing a little out of breath. The door was shut. Célita felt her bag heavy in her hand, a rectangular bag as big as Madame Florence's, which was a kind of sign of her profession; whenever she was not going home to Place du Commandant-Maria for the night, it could hold all her toilet articles and even a nightdress.

Since she was hesitating, Marie-Lou gave her a little shove, and they went through into the hall, where a dim electric light was burning and there was a smell of hot wax and flowers.

The bedroom, where the curtains had been drawn across the windows, was hung in black. The bed and the wardrobe with the mirrors had been removed; there was nothing left but a stand of some sort, covered with a cloth—perhaps the table from the dining room?—supporting the oak coffin with its heavy silver ornamentation.

Each of the two women dipped a twig of box in the holy water and made the sign of the cross in the air, then stood there motionless, as if praying, their lips moving, not daring to look around too much.

Several dark figures were disclosed in the dancing light of the candles: Monsieur Léon, his sister Alice, a man who was presumably her husband, two women they didn't know, and a shrunken little old lady, who looked like a church chair attendant.

It was Madame Florence's mother, who had never been mentioned at the Monico, but had now come down from her village in Berry, where she made cheese from the milk of her goats.

They could not see Maud there. Nobody knew whether she would be at the funeral. As they went out, they touched Léon's hand, mumbling unintelligible syllables meant for condolences, and they were almost surprised to find the sun shining outside and hear the noises of the street.

Marie-Lou and Francine, who suspected nothing, were left wondering when Célita said to them:

"I'll be back in a minute."

They watched her almost run to the corner of the street and disappear into a bar.

"What's bitten her?"

"I don't know," Marie-Lou replied. "The last two days she's been up and down all the time, crying one minute, laughing out loud the next, and then not saying a single word, as if she was hiding something."

And Francine sighed:

"She's always been so melodramatic."

They would surely have been still more anxious had they seen Célita hurriedly swallow two glasses of cognac, while keeping an eye on the street.

The day after Madame Florence's death, the telephone had rung about four o'clock in the afternoon, and Célita had answered it while Marie-Lou went on eating; they had just sat down to lunch.

"Yes, speaking . . ." she'd said, with surprise.

At the other end of the line a voice she did not recognize had mysteriously announced:

"This is Mademoiselle Motta. Do you remember me?"

"No."

"You saw me yesterday. I was the nurse who was looking after Madame Tourmaire. Are you alone?"

Célita had hesitated, then answered:

"Yes."

"I've been asked to give you a message and I wanted to do it without saying a word to anybody else. A few minutes before she died, Madame Tourmaire muttered:

" 'Tell Célita that I'm depending on her. . . .'

"When I asked her what she meant, she added:

" 'Just tell her that; she'll understand.'

"That was all. I've given you the message. It was my duty, I suppose."

She had hung up, and Célita had told Marie-Lou nothing when she looked at her inquiringly. Ten minutes later, however, as if a thought had been pursuing her the whole time, she had exclaimed:

"It's fantastic!"

"What is?"

"Nothing. You wouldn't understand, and anyhow it's too late!"

"Too late for what?"

"Nothing, Marie-Lou, you fool. Forget it!"

From that time on she had been strange. At times she would stare in front of her as if she were seeing things nobody else could see, and she looked like a sleepwalker.

Francine was right: Célita had always been melodramatic, not only with other people, but with herself, and it was probably true that she needed to play certain roles, or exaggerate her own, because she could not put up with life as it really was.

Nobody could have any inkling of her decision, or know that all that was happening now at 57 Boulevard Carnot, and the ceremony of prayers of intercession for the deceased, which would shortly take place, with the organ and incense, in the dimly lit church, followed by the funeral procession across town, was but the prologue to a final scene that Célita, and she alone, had planned, because it was the only one, in her eyes, that was possible.

Had Madame Florence had any idea that her message would arrive too late? Célita had held out as long as possible; the situation could still have been saved when she slapped Léon in the street, with Emile looking on. But not now.

There were certain things he should never have said. He had not thrown her out, but even that was a sign of his contempt, all the more unbearable because it meant he was simply not bothering to do so, being convinced that she would finally walk out of her own accord. Who knows? Perhaps, by waiting, he had grown angry that she was still there, as a kind of witness.

Maybe he would get tired of Maud, as Madame Florence had apparently believed, or else, as Ludo had predicted, Maud would be the one to leave, to climb one more rung of the ladder, as soon as she had the opportunity. In any case, that would take weeks, even months, and whatever the final outcome, Léon would only loathe Célita all the more.

He was the one she hated, because she had humbled herself in vain to get him in her clutches, because he despised her for doing so, never realizing that Maud's game was even more disgusting.

Yet it would have to be on Maud that Célita got her revenge; she was convinced that this was the best means to hurt him, to make him suffer for a long time, to force him to remember her for the rest of his life.

She knew that if she told anybody what she was about to

do, nobody would believe her capable of it, not even Marie-Lou, who lived with her.

For three days, she had been growing more excited, though almost cold-bloodedly. Things would not necessarily be all so gloomy in the future she was planning for herself; she was still capable of calculation, even of fairly cynical calculation.

Once Maud Le Roy was dead, Célita would be put in prison, of course, and it would be an enormous relief for her to find peace at last enclosed by four walls and not to have to think any more. Although she foresaw, in this way, the consequences of her action, she was concerned about its external repercussions: what the newspapers would print, how dumbfounded the people at the Monico would be, and, above all, the way Léon would react.

Wouldn't he realize, at last, that the episode the previous Christmas had not been just a poor piece of playacting?

They would not condemn her to death, for this would be a crime passionnel if ever there was one. If she weren't acquitted—and she had not much hope of that—she would get away with a not very long term, five years perhaps, and the chances were that Léon would come and visit her while she was in prison.

Célita allowed herself a smile now and then at the thought that she was, after all, going to carry out the proprietress's dying wish, though in a way Madame Florence had not foreseen.

The material preparations had taken two days. She knew that it would be impossible, without formalities that were out of the question for her, to buy a revolver at a gunsmith's, and she could not think of anyone to borrow one from. But she knew where to find one: at the Monico, of all places, in one of the drawers below the cash register, where Léon had put it last autumn after there had been armed robberies at two establishments on the Riviera.

The club was closed. The photographs of the naked girls had been taken away temporarily, and a black-edged notice announced: "Closed owing to bereavement."

She had telephoned several times. Now that the proprietor had stopped going to the club regularly every afternoon, Emile had been given a key, so that he could open it for the char-women and the delivery men.

For a day and a half, the telephone had kept ringing with no reply, and she didn't know Emile's address at Le Cannet. Nor did she find him on the Croisette, because he had given up distributing fliers.

The second day, about six, after having telephoned in vain at four, she pushed the door on the off chance, and it opened, almost knocking over Emile, who was squatting down to pick up the letters the postman had pushed through the slit in the door.

"It's you!" he said, surprised, as he stood up.

"I've come to collect one or two things I need."

"It's lucky for you the boss just sent me over to collect the letters. I only got here a minute ago."

The shutters were closed and it was dark, which was lucky too, because Célita was not sure how best to play her role.

"I'm going upstairs for a moment."

Then, as she was pushing open the door with the peephole:

"You wouldn't go and buy me a pack of cigarettes, would you?"

She could not think of any other way to be rid of him, and she sighed with relief when, not suspecting a thing, Emile went off, whistling.

She had brought a screwdriver in case the drawer was locked, as it probably would be. The tobacconist's was not far, and Emile always walked quickly.

The lock gave way immediately. Nobody had removed the short-barreled revolver, so she hurriedly hid it in her bag.

She did not have time, however, to leave the bar. As Emile came in, she picked up a bottle of whisky.

"Any objection?"

"Of course not."

"Do you want some?"

"You know that burns my stomach. Even wine does."

He watched her climb the stairs to the dressing room, and then return with a dress over her arm.

"Mademoiselle Célita . . ."

"I'm in a hurry, Emile."

"It's not what you think."

"I know. . . . I'll see you tomorrow."

And she did see him, when he greeted them but did not dare join their group. The hearse drew up in front of the house, the undertaker's men climbed the stairs, and then reappeared carrying the coffin on their shoulders.

"Do you think she'll come?"

Célita, suddenly furious, looked at Marie-Lou, who, of course, could not understand how her entire plan was based on Maud's presence at the funeral.

Léon came through the door, dressed in black, with a stiff, very white collar and a black tie, which gave him the air of a headwaiter and revealed for the first time—God knows why—that his nose was slightly crooked and one eye was higher than the other.

Beside him trotted the little old lady with the wrinkled face; then, together, came Alice, her husband, and Maud, also in black, even to her hat and gloves. She looked like a member of the family.

They waited a little longer in the sunshine, while people on the street stopped to watch them form into a procession. Ludo, Gianini, and the musicians took their places; Emile, without losing sight of Célita, sidled in beside old Jules; then, haphazardly, came Léon's colleagues, who all knew each other, some tradesmen, also acquainted, and a few strangers.

The parish church was at the top of the boulevard, but Léon had insisted that the service take place at Notre-Dame, near the Monico, probably because it was the town's fashionable church. The hearse was laden with wreaths. One of them, for which a collection had been made, bore a card with the words:

To our dear departed employer
THE STAFF

It had been Ludo's suggestion; he knew the way things were done.

Léon, hat in hand, walked with his head bowed, and Célita noticed that his hair was getting thin. Maud was just behind him; like Alice's, her eyes were red and from time to time she dabbed at her face with a handkerchief. The little old lady, even though she was the dead woman's mother, looked around inquisitively at this town she had not seen before and which she was unlikely to have the opportunity to revisit.

Célita was calm, a little tense, but calm. She had been thinking very hard. Now that she had made her decision and had planned for the slightest detail that might occur, it was almost as if she was no longer concerned with the business at all, as if she had started a mechanism that would now work without her. Like Madame Florence's mother, she found herself staring at things in the street, then at the church as they entered it, the same church from which, not so long ago, she had watched a bride leaving.

The two charwomen, Madame Blanc and Madame Touzelli, were already there, kneeling in the pew second from the back; it was clear they were used to it. Marie-Lou also knew when to cross herself, genuflect, stand up or sit down, have her collection money ready, and Célita watched her, to follow her example.

There was no Mass, only a service of intercession, and the church was more than half full. When they left, people pressed forward on both sides of the porch, almost as inquisitive as at a wedding.

Célita found it all unreal, like a painting, or more like a film when the sound track suddenly fails. She could hardly recognize Léon in his mourning clothes, a suit he had bought ready-made, which was too tight across the shoulders. He was starting to get a potbelly. He had cut himself shaving, and there was still a little red mark on his cheek.

She preferred not to look at Maud, whom the people walking in front of her concealed most of the time, since she wasn't tall. The hearse drove very slowly, and the cortege made its way toward the Carnot bridge, blocking traffic for a while, then went along Rue de Grasse, climbing slowly toward Les Broussailles, where the cemetery was, not far from the new hospital.

There were fewer people than there had been on the way to the church, and two men left the procession to rush off to a bistro for a quick drink. They returned to their places wiping their mouths.

"Do you believe in heaven and hell?" Marie-Lou asked out of the blue, impressed by the intercession service.

Célita did not answer, but the question disturbed her slightly. She preferred not to think about it, particularly now.

She was past going back. Her pride in herself was at stake. She had pictured every possible outcome, and there was no time to go over it again.

"I often wonder . . ."

"Shut up, will you?"

She had said it so harshly that Marie-Lou and Francine looked at her with astonishment. They should have learned to expect almost anything from her.

They were approaching too fast now, along emptier streets, with the splash of color made by a local shop seen only at rare intervals.

She refused to ask herself why she had made her decision. She just *had* to, and that was that! She would do it whatever happened. She could feel the weight of the revolver in her handbag. Nothing else mattered to her any more.

She glimpsed Maud's face as she turned around to look at the procession, and for an instant their eyes met. Strangely, Maud was the first to look away, embarrassed. Had she persuaded Léon to fire Célita? If so, she would no longer have any enemies at the Monico, since Marie-Lou and Francine hardly counted. They were soft. Anyway, Francine had just told them that it was fixed: She was going away for a month with Pierrot, to the mountains, and she wasn't sure whether she would return to the Monico. A businessman from Grasse, who came to see her once or twice a week, and whom Pierrot already called "Uncle," was eager to keep her permanently.

The women's heels twisted on the uneven cobblestones of the uphill street. They passed by old villas and large mansions that had had their heyday when Cannes was still a winter resort and were now converted into flats. The cross, carried by a choirboy, wavered above their heads. They were now approaching the cemetery, passing brand-new tombstones stacked along the sidewalk.

The priest began to chant his prayers again.

"What's the matter?"

"Nothing. I nearly fell."

It was true. Her head was going around as if she were on a swing at the fair; everything she saw was becoming blurred in the sunshine.

They followed well-trodden paths, then more recent ones, and the procession stopped not far from a wall, the cross silhouetted against the sky at the end of its long black wooden pole. In the midst of the dark figures, there appeared a rectangular hole in the yellowish earth.

She had to do it, that was all!

She had thought things over beforehand. Later she would perhaps think things over again. For the moment, she had ceased to exist.

She knew only that she must slip between two men who were standing in the front row, since she had decided to do her deed at the very moment when, the coffin lowered, Léon started throwing in the first shovelful of soil.

"Sorry . . ." murmured one of the men she was pushing, as he stepped back to make room for her.

Maud was in full view, opposite her. She had taken her place next to Léon, as if ready to comfort him with a squeeze of the hand.

The gravediggers had begun work, their faces sweating. As the coffin was being lowered, supported by ropes, it stopped for a moment, as if it had met an obstacle, then started descending again.

Célita opened her bag with her right hand. It disappeared inside, felt the revolver, seized the grip.

Nobody was paying any attention to her. She would have time to take aim. Barely three yards separated her from Maud; there was nothing between them.

"Libera me, Domine . . ."

The liturgical phrases became but a murmur when they were drowned by the noise of a concrete mixer somewhere outside the cemetery.

Célita's clammy hand still clasped the grip of the revolver in her bag; her index finger probed, searched for the trigger, found it.

She stared at Maud, and was suddenly bewildered, as if she was no longer conscious of where she was or what she was doing. Did she even still know who the young girl was who was looking down into the hole and why she was going to kill her?

Somebody handed Léon a shovel, with a little earth on it, and he bent down awkwardly. Célita, noticed by nobody, took the revolver from her bag.

Now it was not Maud at whom she aimed. She raised the gun slowly, the muzzle turned toward herself. Panic had overcome her; there was no other solution but to kill herself.

All she had to do was raise her arm slightly, turn her wrist.

Then it would be over. There would be no more problems, no more unpleasantness or humiliation, no more Célita, nothing any more.

Léon was straightening up again, his face crimson, looking about him, wondering if there was anything else he had to do, and his eyes rested on Célita, on the gun she was holding in her hand.

Then, without thinking, without realizing how theatrical her action would seem, she threw the revolver into the grave and, pushing through the crowd, began running down the paths, convinced she was being chased, searching for the way out. When she found it, she started off down the steep street leading to town, her eyes mad.

Chapter Nine

Marie-Lou was the only one of the old bunch left. Francine had gone away the day after the funeral, and they had had one new girl, from Marseille, then another, an Italian whose name could not be announced on the fliers because she hadn't got her work permit yet.

Alice, the proprietor's sister, had returned to Le Havre, because her husband needed her, and a former cashier from the Café des Allées had been hired.

Léon continued to bring Maud and take her back after her performance. He was living at the Louxor now, going only occasionally to Boulevard Carnot, to get some of his belongings.

It was Ludo who got indirect news of Célita and passed it on to Marie-Lou. The fat girl had taken the Italian to share the flat on Place du Commandant-Maria, because it was too expensive for her alone.

"She's been seen in Nice," he told her one evening. "Apparently she was in a small bar, with Ketty. . . ."

Marie-Lou was too upset to say anything. For her, and for Ludo as well, those words could mean only one thing.

A few days later, a regular customer also mentioned her. He had seen her standing in a doorway, near a hotel.

The season was in full swing. The cars were almost bumper to bumper and took an hour to drive the length of the Croisette. Women appeared even on Rue d'Antibes in bikinis; Marie-Lou had seen a woman, at least sixty, wearing one in the pharmacy.

The end came, as they learned from the newspaper, a few days before August 15.

The body of an entirely naked woman, covered with bruises, "which might have been due to its being repeatedly buffeted against the rocks," had been recovered from the sea between Nice and Villefranche.

Two days later, *Nice-Matin* announced that the corpse had been identified as "one Céline Perrin, single, age thirty-two, born in Paris, Rue Caulaincourt, cabaret dancer, who had been summoned twice by the police during the last few days for soliciting on the streets."

Finally:

"Investigations are being carried out in certain special areas of the town, particularly among North Africans, because the dead woman's handbag and clothes have not been found, and three days before the discovery of the body, Céline Perrin had been seen in the company of an Arab whose description is in the hands of the police."

"Do you think she'd do that, Ludo?"

The bartender looked at Marie-Lou without replying, sighed, took a bottle of cognac from the shelf and poured himself a full glass, exactly as he had done for Madame Florence.

"Give me some too."

Then she began to say:

"If she did that, I think she . . ."

But what was the use of talking?

She emptied her glass in one gulp, because the proprietor was making signs to her to go and change for her number.

12 June 1957